Blitz

The Storm Dragons' Mate

M. Sinclair

Lost & Bound Publishing

Blitz: The Storm Dragons' Mate 1

Copyright © 2022 by M. Sinclair in USA

Refined Voice Editing & Proofreading

Cover: Emily Wittig

 Created with Vellum

The Union of Love & Madness

Description

Three dominant dragon alphas who seemingly have it all... except the one thing they want: *me*.

My life hasn't been typical. All I remember is waking up in an alley when I was ten, scrounging for scraps to survive until I was taken to the Bronzeheart estate.

That's where my life began, where I've lived for the past eight years with the ruling family, the Blitz Clan. It's where I found my best friend Gage, the future leader of this clan.

At the time, I didn't question my good fortune because I was happy to know I wasn't alone in this world anymore. But maybe I should have.

After landing a shocking invite to the prestigious

Dark Imaginarium Academy, I realized how much of a safe haven the estate was.

The students at this school are out for my blood because somehow I have the attention of not just one, but all three Storm Dragon Clan heirs: Gage Bronzeheart, Breaker Firespell, and Jagger Silvershade.

None of them should have an interest in me, seeing as I'm the only shifter at this academy who hasn't, you know...shifted. They should want someone powerful at their side. But it doesn't stop me from wanting them as well.

That is until I find out they've been hiding a life-changing secret from me. And now that I know...

Nothing will be the same.

Blitz is book 1 in the Storm Dragons' Mate trilogy that features a slightly naive but sassy MFC, possessive dragon alphas, and a secret that will change everything. This is not a high school academy book and the contents are intended for mature audiences, with characters who are all 18+. This book includes violence and mature sexual content.

Author Note:

Blitz is set in the shared universe of Dark Imaginarium Academy. All series can be read independently, but characters have crossovers and it is highly encouraged to read all within the universe to understand the world in its entirety.

Series within the universe:

Phases of the Moon by M. Sinclair

The Creatures We Crave by R.L. Caulder

The Storm Dragons' Mate by M. Sinclair

Blood Oath by R.L. Caulder (Coming soon)

Prologue

Bexley

I *was so cold.*

I'd never been this cold in my life...at least I didn't think I had. I honestly couldn't remember. My brain felt fuzzy, and everything hurt, right down to my frozen fingertips. As if that wasn't enough, my stomach kept cramping in pain.

I was so hungry. So incredibly hungry. It made the world spin around me as I tried to sort through the pile of discarded food at my feet where I was crouched.

How many days had I been out here alone?

I could only remember the past few hours, so there was really no way to tell. It felt like a long time though. More importantly, why couldn't I remember anything before that? How had I gotten here in the first place? Had someone left me?

I examined my shiny shoes, which laced up my ankles, and the sparkly skirt of my dress that fell to my knees. The material was expensive and looked practically brand new. I didn't think I lived on the streets. At least, not usually. I mean, why else would I be dressed like I was going to a party? I tried to think back to how I even knew that and slammed into a solid wall that caused pain to radiate through my temples.

A whimper slipped through my lips. *It wasn't worth it.* That was the silent whisper that slipped into my head, warning me that it would cause me far more pain to push through my memories than to simply let it go. I wanted to do that, I wanted to believe that...but there was another part of me that knew this was wrong.

Something about this entire situation felt wrong.

When a cool, wet wind ran over my skin, my stomach made another sound of protest, insisting that we were hungry. Inspecting the food in front of me, I stared at the half-eaten sandwich that someone had thrown out.

Like you. Someone had thrown it out like they threw you out.

That painful reminder tugged at a part of me that had my eyes watering. I sniffed, trying to calm myself down as my mouth watered from staring at the piece of food. My hand moved forward to grab it but stopped short. I didn't want to eat this. I knew that. But I also knew I wouldn't be able to focus on figuring out where I was supposed to go, or what had happened, if I couldn't see straight because of hunger.

Before I could touch the sandwich, a loud screech sounded, and I immediately jolted up, looking towards the end of the alleyway. I blinked in confusion, wrapping my arms around myself, noticing a gorgeous black car that now blocked the entrance. I didn't feel panic at the intrusion; something about the vehicle was familiar. I took a hesitant step towards it before the door flew open and revealed a young boy who looked about my age, maybe slightly older. I stood still, not knowing if I should approach him, though something in my head and heart was urging me to do exactly that.

Then he called out, "Bexley? Is that you?"

Bexley? Was that my name? I hesitantly took a step towards him but froze as the front door of the car opened to reveal an older man. I looked between the two of them, realizing they looked startlingly similar. Maybe that was the boy's father?

Did I have a father? A mother? My temples pounded in pain, warning me that those thoughts were off-limits.

"Bex?" the boy said again in a softer voice, as if he was worried about scaring me. His voice was nice, welcoming, and almost familiar, echoing through the dirty alleyway.

"I...I don't know who you are looking for. I don't know my name," I admitted softly. The boy was there then, right in front of me faster than the blink of an eye, looking both relieved and panicked. I stared at him, completely shocked to find such intense green eyes looking down at me as his arms wrapped around my own.

"I was so worried." His voice was saturated with emotion, and tears filled his eyes. "I thought that you were gone forever. We couldn't find you, and when we heard about—"

Pain detonated through my temples as he continued to talk to me, his words blurring together to become one stream of incoherent sounds. *Heard about what? What was he hearing about? What did that have to do with me?*

I whimpered, clinging to him tightly as tears streamed down my face, not knowing how else to deal with this level of pain. I knew he stopped talking when my head stopped hurting. When he said something about me being cold, he pulled back and wrapped a jacket around me, surrounding me in warmth.

His voice finally broke through the haze I was feeling when he shouted, "Dad, something is wrong with Bex! She's crying!"

The older man appeared next to us, gently prying my hands away from my face as I tried to rub away the tears. "Bexley?"

I looked up at him, and something about my expression caused him to look concerned. He spoke softer this time. "Do you know who you are?"

"No," I whispered, my voice filled with fear. "Is that my name? I can't—I can't remember anything. I've been out here for a day, I think? Maybe more."

"Let's get her in the car," the boy's father insisted. He was trying to remain calm, but I could see my fear mimicked in his gaze.

I nodded, and the boy put his arm around me and ushered me towards the large car, comfort and security suffusing me as I leaned into him. I could feel that my eyes were still watering, but where I had felt fear moments ago, I now only felt exhaustion.

How did these people know who I was?

What had happened to put me into this situation?

My breathing went a bit rough, feeling the overwhelming enormity of this situation hit me as we neared the car. I was put into a large leather seat, the heat of the car blasting against my skin instantly filling me with relief. A large blanket was wrapped around my shoulders, over the jacket, and the father was shouting orders to someone at the front of the car before we even drove away. I kept my face buried against the boy's chest, not wanting to fully deal with whatever was going on.

"What's your name?" I finally asked, tilting my head back.

Sadness filled his eyes, making me feel like I'd asked something horrible. "You don't remember me?"

"I don't remember anything."

He hugged me fiercely. "I swear, Bex, we will figure out what happened. You're safe now. I promise that you are completely safe. Dad, she's safe, right? We are taking her back to the estate?"

"Yes," his father promised, sounding tense and upset. "We are taking her back home. I am going to have a doctor brought in just to make sure she hasn't been injured. Are you in pain at all, Bexley?"

"No," I croaked. "My head just hurts... And I'm confused. What is going on?"

The boy's father met my gaze, sadness radiating through his expression as he opened his mouth to speak. I couldn't tell you what he said, though, because the minute he began talking, pain exploded through my head. Agony tore through me and I cried out, my entire body jolting. My eyes fell shut, and I fell into the darkness knowing that something terrible had happened...

I just couldn't remember what.

Chapter 1

Bexley

The afternoon sunlight streamed down on my head as I tucked my jacket further around me, smoothing my fingers over the small note I'd been waiting for all week. I always knew when it would be arriving, almost like an internal clock, and today, after Gage had gone off to his meeting, I'd taken a long stroll through the estate's far-extending lands until I hit the southernmost wall.

That was where I'd found my note, buried in the soft earth at the base of a rose bush. My fingers had a tiny bit of dirt on them, but it didn't stop me from opening the note and smiling at the messy scrawl.

Today changes everything.

. . .

What did they mean by that? The notes I received were usually brief as it was, but this was particularly short. Over the years, since finding the first one, I'd always written back far more extensive replies, especially when my secret pen pal asked questions. Of course, I would ask questions in return, but it was very rare, if ever, that I got a response back, unfortunately.

I was hoping one day I would receive a letter that had all of them answered, pages so thick that I ended up knowing as much about my pen pal as they knew about me. A small sigh left my lips as I folded the note back up and tucked it into the pocket of my skirt.

It was a gorgeous day out, and I wasn't in any particular rush to go inside. I could practically scent autumn in the air, and while I loved the seasonal change, there was a small part of me that was sad. I knew Gage would soon be leaving for school once again, and despite having taken the exam at the start of summer to join him this fall, I'd heard no word from the Dark Imaginarium Academy.

No one said it directly, but I was almost positive I hadn't gotten in. Honestly, I wasn't very surprised. I mean, I had never shifted. What else would I expect?

A sad hum left my lips, but before I could get down

in the dumps, a gorgeous butterfly with glittery gold and silver wings floated past me. I sat perfectly still, hoping that it would land on me. I knew that it was unlikely, but I still stretched out my finger, offering it a perfect place to land.

Much to my surprise, it did exactly that, and my chest squeezed happily. I had always loved butterflies. I had also envied their ability to fly for far too long, although that wasn't exactly shocking. I was surrounded by dragons; how could I not be envious? I couldn't imagine the freedom associated with such a luxury.

"Ms. Bexley." A soft-spoken familiar voice had me looking up to see Mr. Webb approaching, his appearance causing my butterfly to go airborne. I followed it with my eyes before offering a friendly smile to our estate's head steward. This morning he was dressed in a navy outfit accented with a gold pocket watch that hung prominently at his hip, flashing in the sun with every step. I tried to not focus too much on it, but I had a bad addiction to things that were shiny or glittery. It was a fact at this point.

"Good afternoon, Mr. Webb," I greeted happily.

"Delivery," he offered, handing me a large, thick envelope. I frowned slightly in confusion as he offered me a wink and turned around, departing down the same path he'd arrived on. I stared down at the parcel in my hand, nerves hitting me, feeling as though I'd manifested my thoughts into being or that the fates had heard me. My hand trembled as I inspected the elegant scripted font of my name on the ivory-colored envelope. Up top, there was a crest that was traditional in nature. One that I recognized...

I pulled the envelope to my chest, hopped up, and strode through the garden towards the breezeway that connected my suite to the rest of the house. *Holy fates.* There was no way, right? I mean, there was only one possible source of this letter. I just had assumed it was never coming, and now that I had it in my hands, I wasn't positive I was ready to open it and see their response.

The Dark Imaginarium Academy's decision on whether I was admitted or not.

I drew in a breath as I arrived in my suite, swinging open the door and not bothering to close it. I bit my bottom lip nervously. How the heck was I supposed to open this up on my own? I looked back towards the long stone breezeway that led to the main house, the early afternoon glow that came through painting the entire place in a peaceful gold light that was not echoed by my current mental state.

I fought the urge to go to the main house to find

someone to join me in this important moment because I knew there wasn't anyone home right now.

Well, that wasn't completely true—Gage and his father were home, they were just in an important meeting. One that I couldn't interrupt despite desperately wanting to. I stared at the envelope, standing in the middle of my large suite as I frowned. Why was I getting this now? I had somewhat accepted that I hadn't gotten in, and now it was possible I would have to go through the rejection again.

There was nothing I wanted more than to join Gage at DIA, so if I didn't get in and I had to see that written out, I had a feeling it would break my heart a bit.

Placing down the letter, I left it on the elegant long table that filled the center of my suite. There were fresh daisies placed in a large vase in vibrant shades of red, orange, and yellow, filling the room with a soft floral scent. They were delivered fresh each day, and despite never admitting to it, it was one of my favorite parts of this space.

Well, that and everything else about it.

I looked around the grand yet comfortable room, wondering if I was truly ready to leave this place. If I was truly ready to take this next step of my journey... That is, on the off chance I got in, which was still extremely unlikely in my mind.

The Bronzeheart estate was all I knew now, and the way I'd been brought up here far exceeded anything I could have expected out of my life—after all, I'd literally been found in an alleyway scrounging for scraps.

Thinking of that night caused my head to pulse, so I pushed past the memory. Not only was it painful emotionally, but physically as well. It was why everyone avoided talking about it around me. The doctors thought that it was some form of post-traumatic stress associated with whatever happened to me, a mystery we had yet to solve.

So I kept it from my head.

Still, how I had gone from that to having an entire section of the estate to myself was mind-blowing. The gorgeous arched white ceilings, which were embellished with hand-painted gold details, framed large windows on all sides that showcased the natural beauty of the garden that surrounded my area of the grounds.

A far cry from an alleyway, to say the least.

Green dotted with warm tones decorated the landscape outside, and I walked away from the envelope, opening the french doors that led to my small patio and breathing in the fresh air, trying to calm myself. After a minute of taking a deep inhale and then exhaling, I realized it was pointless. I groaned and turned back towards the letter, narrowing my eyes at it as if it was the true enemy here and not my own thoughts.

I just needed to open it.

So why did the idea of laying out on the luxurious furniture around me sound so much more appealing? *Because this was home.* The Bronzeheart estate was my home and my safe place. Why would I ever want to leave?

My face heated. I knew why. While the estate was indeed home, there was one person who made it that way. *Gage Bronzeheart.* My best friend, who happened to be a year older than me, had been attached to my side since he found me in that alleyway.

I frowned slightly, the memory of that night surging forward again, as it had done more frequently lately. Just the other day, on my birthday, I had woken up crying, with the memory of everything that had happened that night and feeling a swell of confusion that I wasn't used to at all. More than that though, I'd found that I could think about that night with more clarity than before. It still hurt, but the level of fuzziness that had been obscuring certain facts had all but disappeared. An instinctual part of me told me to keep pushing past the pain to think through that night... I just rebelled so hard against that notion because of the debilitating effects doing so had caused in the past.

It was a mystery that needed to be solved, though. There were too many questions about my past left unanswered.

One of the most confusing aspects? It felt like Gage had known me, like Mr. Bronzeheart had known me, when they found me in that alley... I just didn't understand how that was possible. The few times I'd tried to ask, or even thought too hard about it, I ended up in pure head-splitting agony, so one could understand why I was hesitant to dive back into it again.

As for attending the academy, don't get me wrong, there were a million reasons why I wanted to attend such a prestigious school... But the idea of seeing Gage every day? Seeing his gorgeous smile every morning like before he left for school? The concept had my heart pumping fast and a sense of warm contentment running through my system. It was always the reaction I had to thoughts of Gage... Well, that and other ones that would completely ruin our friendship.

Which was why I needed to focus on opening this freakin' letter.

"Ms. Bex?" A soft, feminine voice called out my name. I looked towards the door to find Ms. Payne standing there with her pushcart and trays. I crossed the room and slid the letter further down the table, not wanting to draw attention to it.

Ms. Bex. I nearly smiled at that. I had insisted that she call me Bex instead of Bexley, but she had refused to drop the 'Ms.,' so I figured it was the best compromise I would get. I had also insisted that it wasn't necessary for her to bring me lunch, that I could go to the kitchen, but I knew she enjoyed coming to spend time with me. She was a bit older and didn't have any family that lived on the estate with her, so I figured she grew a bit lonely sometimes.

Plus, we bonded over knitting after she'd introduced me to the calming activity.

"Good afternoon, Ms. Payne," I sang happily.

"What's that?" she asked curiously, nodding towards the letter as I took the food from her, setting it down on the table. I also grabbed the iced coffee, taking a long sip before sitting down at one of the chairs, motioning for her to join me.

"It's nothing important—crap," I muttered as she ignored me and walked around the table, picking up the thick envelope and offering me a questioning look.

"The academy?" she asked as I took another long sip of my iced coffee.

She knew I wouldn't lie to her—I couldn't lie to save my life. It was horrible when I was trying to get away with anything or plan surprises. *Four times.* I'd tried four times to surprise Gage with everything from a special edition car he'd wanted to a party celebrating his admittance into DIA, but every time he would ask me what was going on, I would stumble over my excuses until I finally gave in. He said it was adorable, and I absolutely did not agree.

I was just glad he had never found my little box of notes I kept from my pen pal. It was the only secret I had kept from him outside of my feelings... And if he asked, I would one hundred percent tell him everything. My chest squeezed with the guilt of not telling him something. It wasn't that I didn't want to tell him, it's just that this felt personal. No, intimate. It felt like an intimate conversation.

"The academy," I confirmed in defeat.

"Why are you waiting to open it?" she asked softly, an understanding note to her voice, as she leaned forward against the back of a chair across from me.

"It's just a bit nerve-wracking," I expressed.

I wasn't afraid to admit that. This letter and the decision inside meant so much for my future. Don't get me wrong, I knew that the Bronzeheart family would always keep me protected and safe, but there was something about taking direct control of my life that felt important. There were a lot of things in my life that weren't in my control, so this felt right. *Scary, but right.*

I reached for the envelope as she handed it to me. "I

assumed I didn't get in. It's been all summer... And now that I have it, I just don't know what I'll do if they've rejected me." Which was a completely reasonable expectation.

Why would a prestigious academy's shifter sector admit a girl with no family name? Better yet, why would they let in a shifter who'd never shifted before? Who didn't even know what their animal counterpart was? Honestly, the more I'd thought about it this summer, the more I realized that the chances of me getting in were extremely low. Maybe it would be better for someone else to open the letter for me. I wasn't positive I wanted to be part of the process at all now.

Although... I hid my face in my hands. How embarrassing would it be if I had Gage open it for me and I didn't get in? Pulling out of my thoughts, I looked up at Ms. Payne, who stared at me with sympathy.

"I can tell you're worked up about this. Why don't you eat some lunch, and I'll make some cupcakes—how does that sound?"

Her method of providing comfort had me instantly smiling. "I can never say no to cupcakes," I replied happily. She offered me a big smile, seemingly content that she made me feel better, as she pushed the food cart back out of my room and down the long hall. I took another long sip of my iced coffee before shaking my head. I was being ridiculous. I couldn't avoid this forever.

The sound of bells distracted me briefly as I trailed towards the windows near the back of the room, noticing that a motorcade of black cars had pulled up.

The staff greeted the guests, a series of rather tall, intimidating older men, and led them towards the main entrance of the house. I had a feeling Gage's meeting today would be an extensive one for sure.

The Bronzeheart men—Gage's father, and now himself—were always busy. As the leaders of the Blitz Clan, one of three Storm Dragon Clans of our territory, Trabea, they not only lived in a world essentially removed from normal shifters, even other dragons, but were solely focused on protecting their clan and the other shifters that lived under their protection. It was a full-time job, and I had slowly watched my best friend transform from the boy who played in the gardens with me to a man that would soon govern an entire sector of Trabea.

My skin prickled at that, trying to not delve into why that type of power and dominance was so attractive to me. Then again, *everything* about Gage was attractive to me.

However, because I'd sat sideline to all of this, I had grown used to the level of wealth that had surprised me upon arrival. Although, it hadn't surprised me that much...at least not as much as I would have assumed. Rather than being cold and unwelcoming, I had found comfort in the gleam of expensive marble and crystal, always finding something to admire and explore. I'd easily transitioned into this lifestyle, and now I couldn't imagine living any other way.

See? Even if I didn't get into DIA, there were some positive aspects! Like my life not having to change. And then my communication with my pen pal wouldn't have to stop! I couldn't imagine not communicating with them. I had noticed that during the year the notes tended to slow down anyway, but this summer there had been an abundance of them. I didn't want that to end.

But I also knew I couldn't live my life waiting on little notes.

If I didn't get in, it wouldn't be the end of the world, but it would be three more years of not seeing Gage every day. I would probably have to find something to do for the family. After all, I'd been raised here and was considered part of the elite Bronzeheart household. They were the only family I knew, and any blood relatives I'd had before obviously had abandoned me, so I wasn't sure I wanted to know them.

Actually, I *knew* I didn't want to know them.

My stomach tightened, realizing that was another

aspect of the academy I needed to worry about. I didn't think there was a way for anyone at the school to know the details of how I'd come to live with the Bronze-hearts, but I also had a feeling that it wouldn't be met with a kind reception if they found out I'd come from squalor.

The Bronzehearts didn't keep me a secret, exactly—in fact, Gage often brought me into town—but I hadn't attended school like other shifters. No, Gage and I had been taught by a private tutor, and on the occasion someone did ask about my background, the Bronze-hearts just explained that I was under their protection.

Leopold and Celine Bronzeheart didn't need to explain themselves to anyone.

This was why I didn't want anyone to find out about my past. I would never want to embarrass them, and I knew it would look bad on them and Gage if anyone found out he was associating with someone of my pedi-gree. No one had ever made me feel that way, but it was one of the darker thoughts that plagued me, usually followed by a sense of deep thankfulness to them and the fates.

Not only for taking me in, but for allowing me to find Gage.

My *only* best friend—something that was purely by choice, for the record. There were other shifters who wanted to be friends with me, ones that I met sometimes at the large functions here, but I had realized long ago that more often than not, all they wanted was to get close to the Bronzeheart family. Either that or Gage would scare them off, insisting they had poor intentions towards me, and of course, I trusted him. He was always looking out for my well-being.

"Bex!"

A smile broke out onto my lips—*speak of the dragon himself.* I quickly grabbed the envelope and hid it behind the flower vase, standing from my chair and taking a long sip of my iced coffee while trying to look casual. We were about to put that lying theory to the test, because I had a feeling Ms. Payne had told him about the letter. And I was determined to open it alone.

Chapter 2

Bexley

When Gage Bronzeheart pushed through the glass doors on the opposite end of the breezeway and strode towards the open doors of my suite, his emerald gaze caught mine. My chest squeezed as I tried to ignore the way my cheeks deepened in color at his full attention, something that had been happening more and more in the past year. Especially since he left for DIA and came back... different. More intense. Slightly darker. Still my best friend, but no longer the boy I'd grown up with. Then again, it was up for debate whether he had actually ever been anything but the gorgeous male shifter coming towards me.

No! Fates, Bexley. Stop thinking like that.

I needed to stop. I should be lucky to have such an

amazing friend, so why were my body and heart insisting on ruining it with all these other feelings and thoughts?

"Aren't you supposed to be in a *very* important meeting?" I teased as I stood, meeting him nearly toe to toe as he appeared right in front of me. I tilted my head back, trying to not look over him too much, but unable to help appreciating how muscular he looked in his current choice of clothing.

As mentioned, in the last year, there were subtle changes that Gage had gone through, and how he dressed was a significant one. Today he was dressed in all black, and his t-shirt, which molded to his perfectly cut and muscular chest, was tucked into black dress pants, the whole thing accented by a bronze belt buckle and black leather shoes. It was a really, really attractive look, and despite being in complete contrast to my own clothing choice, I didn't feel at odds standing next to him. This was just us.

Seriously though, I think everyone at the estate was pretty much used to how I dressed. Today I was wearing an ivory silk dress that featured a tight corset along my chest and waist, with a skirt that hung around my legs and sleeves that fell loosely off my shoulders. I had a light knit shawl that sparkled underneath the sun, and I was barefoot except for a diamond ankle bracelet that wrapped around my right foot. It was actually rather casual in comparison to my normal attire.

Although, you could hardly blame me! Mrs. Bronzeheart was nearly as bad, and she fueled my love for expensive items by randomly having stuff shipped to the estate from across the territory. It was all her fault... Also Gage's, though, because *I* hadn't been the one to purchase the diamonds I was wearing. I also wasn't the one who purchased the white glittering car that sat in the family's garage.

Nope! *Not me...*

But... I had been the one to have the bathroom remodeled so that the bathtub and shower tiles were white with embedded diamonds. Yeah...that part had been me.

"Somewhat, but not nearly as important as this." Gage's expression was knowing as I stepped to the side while he looked around the room. He strode forward, shifting some of my lunch trays around, clearly in search of the letter. I took a sip of my iced coffee, using the moment to watch as he ran a large hand through his richly colored dark hair to push it out of his face.

His arm muscle flexed, and the golden light from the windows highlighted the auburn undertones of his hair and the golden hue to his skin. Fates. He was just... gorgeous. That wasn't even including his beautiful smile and his impressively large 6'6" height, stacked with well-built bulky muscles.

A sigh nearly escaped my lips, once again facing the internal problem of 'why do I find my best friend so attractive?' I mean, I suppose 'why' wasn't in question, but more 'why did I *have* to feel this way?' I moved my gaze back to his face, not wanting to cause an issue like two days ago when I'd made the mistake of staring for a bit too long and inspiring a rather frustrating yet natural reaction in my body... That had been a bit awkward for me when my desire had scented the air.

Gage had reacted a bit differently though—as in, he pinned me against the wall and buried his nose against my throat until he calmed down. Then he had left my room and we had yet to talk about it. So in my mind, had it even really happened?

Who was I kidding. It had.

It had totally happened, and I would never forget how good it felt to be pressed between the wall and him.

Unfortunately, I knew it was just his dragon acting up like always, so I had to try to not take it personally when he just pretended as if it had never occurred. Hadn't worked on my end, but he seemed to have forgotten about it, so that was good. Sort of.

"Not as important as *what*?" I asked curiously as he snapped his gaze back towards me. I was always caught off guard by how much of a difference a foot of height made between us. The man was actually massive. You would think the height levels would have been a bit more equitable between the elite dragons and us common folk, but apparently, the fates disagreed because I felt absolutely shrimpy next to him.

Gage stepped towards me and bent down, offering me a knowing look. His emerald eyes flashed with bronze sparks, a sure sign that his dragon was present. "Where is it?"

"Where is what?" I asked curiously with an arched brow.

"The letter, Bex. Show me the damn letter."

I blinked innocently and shrugged. "Haven't gotten it, why would I get it now? It's been all summer."

"Little liar." He chuckled softly and straightened, turning his back to me as I grabbed the letter from behind the flower vase. "That's fine, I'll find it."

I darted away, letter in hand, and sprinted towards the doors that led to my bedroom. He let out a low growl as I slipped into the luxurious space and slammed the doors shut, leaning against the surface and feeling absolutely proud of myself for avoiding his grasp. When his magic brushed against my skin, nearly overwhelming me from the other side of the door, he spoke with a relaxed tone that didn't match literally anything else about him.

"Hand it over."

"No way." I grinned to myself, tossing the letter on the massive bed near me. "I am not opening it with you here. What if I don't get in? There is a reason it's been all summer, and that would be so embarrassing."

He let out an amused sound. "You got in. I can guarantee it."

I threw open the door and narrowed my eyes up at him. "You better not have said anything to them or used the family name, Gage. I will never forgive you."

I was such a liar.

He put his hands out in an innocent gesture. "I promised I wouldn't. I said 'I will not interfere with your acceptance into the academy.' I didn't break any of your rules, cupcake."

"Good," I murmured, trying to not blush at the nickname he called me so easily. He clearly didn't understand how it affected me, probably viewing it as a joke because of my love for cupcakes, or he wouldn't be calling me it. I really did have a bad addiction to cupcakes, and a not-so-small part of that was because edible glitter was usually mixed into the frosting. If that wasn't cool, what the heck was?

See! Another reason why not getting into the academy could be a good thing. I would miss out on the cupcakes the estate had.

With a huff, I walked towards the bed where the letter lay and sat down on the comfortable surface, Gage coming to crouch down in front of me. I resisted the sudden urge to touch him in any way, a desire that had been growing since he came back from school at the start of the summer. It was nearly unbearable. I completely blamed my nerves about this letter coming my way, my obvious denial for acceptance, and knowing the comfort he could provide.

Not because I wanted to touch his sexy muscles or anything...

"I can't open it." I thrust it into his chest. "You do it, please?"

He shook his head and pressed it gently back towards me. "Open it. Now."

I mumbled a curse, trying to ignore how his command ran over me, as I glared at him while tearing it open. His smile grew at my attempt at being mad at him, which failed horribly since the two of us had never actually had a fight. Well...except for that time he'd stolen my favorite scarf.

Of course, since then he'd bought me a brand new one, almost an exact replica, but he said the other one was officially part of his collection. Something that was really his hoard, despite his denials, and that I couldn't take it back anymore because his dragon wanted it.

I did believe Gage—his dragon was a bit of work and totally liked to take my stuff. In fact, his 'collection' was almost entirely comprised of things that used to belong to me. I wasn't much different, though, considering I'd stolen nearly all of the hoodies he owned, so I couldn't really throw stones. Although his dragon had him doing other stuff as well, like smelling my hair or holding me. It was a bit of an odd dynamic and absolutely wonderful for me. I just wished Gage liked me as much as his dragon did.

"Cupcake," Gage encouraged.

I looked down at the letter, having gotten distracted staring at him, as my shaky fingers pulled out the papers before the envelope fluttered to the floor. I blinked, trying to focus on the words as I unfolded the top piece and read the top line.

Dear Bexley Bronzeheart...

I hesitated, examining my name next to 'Bronzeheart,' and found a giddy excitement building in my chest. Of course, everyone was aware we weren't related—obviously not married either—and I'm sure the school put it because I was registered under the family's estate...but it felt good to see it. It felt right. My cheeks flushed at my ridiculous desires before I tried to refocus on the task at hand.

Congratulations! On behalf of the office of Headmistress Estrid, it is my pleasure to announce your acceptance into the Dark Imaginarium Academy...

Oh. My. Fates.

My mouth dropped open in shock and my eyes went wide as I met Gage's green gaze. His smirk was a bit cocky, but the excitement in his eyes was authentic. I looked down at the letter and then back up at him.

I let out the world's most ridiculous squeak of excitement and threw myself at him, literally tackling him. With a grunt, the two of us tumbled back as I landed on top of him, a groan breaking from his lips. There was no way that I'd knocked him to the ground, but it was still funny he was acting like it. I smiled down at him as I waved the letter in excitement, feeling almost hyper.

"Gage! I got in. I got into freakin' DIA! This is insane, I thought for sure I wouldn't! Especially after all summer—" I was rambling, talking extremely fast, as his eyes shifted from an emerald green into bronze, a relaxed, almost lazy smile appearing on his lips as his hands lightly gripped my hips in stabilization.

The man was an intoxicating mix of confidence and intensity that always had me wondering how he would react next...But right now I couldn't focus on that.

"Are you sure you didn't have anything to do with this?" I asked, switching gears. "I mean, I can't even shift!"

"But you are brilliant," he said seriously, squeezing my hips, the silk material of my dress riding up slightly from where I was straddling him. "I promise this was all you, cupcake."

I let out another ridiculous squeal and pulled the letter into my chest before looking back down at it, reading the top few lines again and again. I knew I should have gotten off of Gage, but considering he was just smoothing his fingers over my hips and I could feel his eyes on me, I felt like we were both comfortable.

"Bex." Gage's voice was a low rumble, rougher than normal, as I met his purely bronze gaze that I knew was largely his dragon. Or at least that was what he told me whenever he got worked up. I didn't really understand how the dragon thing worked after all this time, and it wasn't like I had an animal counterpart of my own to compare it to.

"Let's sit up."

"Sorry!" I immediately shifted off of him—or tried to, sliding back, but his hand tightened on me as if trying to keep me from pushing too far back. I knew it was just him making sure I didn't hurt myself, which was confirmed as he gently lifted and set me down next to him, where I sat on the floor and looked back over the letter again. I was so giddy with excitement that I didn't even realize he was staring at me with a smile on his lips until he tucked a piece of my hair behind my ear.

"Are you happy?" His voice was filled with an emotion I hadn't heard before.

"Of course, I am," I expressed softly. "You know how much I've missed hanging out with you this year."

His eyes, which had softened back to emerald, flashed with bronze for just a moment. I felt my excitement dip as I considered something. "Unless we can't hang out? I know people here understand the situation, but I imagine at the academy they may find it odd since you're a dragon and I'm literally a non-shifted shifter." The ending of my words was teasing, but I still felt anxious at his response.

I continued, wanting to give him an out, "I'm sure I can find friends—"

"No." His voice was hard and absolute, his answer clear, before he seemed to forcibly relax, pulling me fully onto his lap again so that I was tucked against his chest. "Trust me, Bex, there is absolutely nothing that is going to stop us from being together."

I could hear the promise in that. I just wished 'being together' meant more than being friends. I knew he found me attractive to an extent, or at least that was the physical reaction to me—literally one I could feel right this moment—but I didn't think emotionally he saw me that way. And if he did, he had never mentioned it for a reason.

I decided to tease him, looking up at him with a coy smile. "I don't know, Gage. I mean, you might scare off all of my classmates by being so intimidating and menacing. You are, after all, the *prestigious* heir of the Bronzeheart Estate." I offered him my most prim look and 'fancy' voice our steward used when announcing guests. "I don't know if anyone will want to hang out with me with the intimidating future Alpha of the Blitz Clan nearby. This could be a bad idea."

That was completely untrue. In fact, I suspected the opposite, but I loved teasing him about his fancy title because he was so not like that. At least not with me. It was hard to be intimidated by a man who loved to watch cartoons with me on Sunday mornings.

"Good." He flashed a dangerous smile. "They don't matter."

"Okay." I nodded seriously and then sighed, giving

him a small sympathetic pat on his chest. "I suppose I will be your only friend."

His full smile was absolutely gorgeous, and his laugh was wonderful, filling the space and making me sigh like a lovestruck idiot.

I swallowed and looked down at the letter. "Gage... This has been an amazing week, this letter and turning eighteen in the span of forty-eight hours. What is going to happen next?"

"That is part of the reason I'm here," he offered in a tone that seemed to be almost hiding something, his eyes darkening. "I finally have your gift."

"You already gave me a gift," I teased, remembering the morning of my eighteenth birthday. My entire suite had been filled with gifts from Gage and his parents. I'd spent the morning outside enjoying an extravagant brunch and then the rest of the day relaxing with them before the dinner party they'd thrown me. It hadn't been necessary—none of it had—but I still loved that they cared about me enough to plan something special for a day that I hadn't even realized was sneaking up on me.

"This is the special one," he promised, standing up. I followed, watching as Gage took out a square box that almost appeared to be one that you would get from a jeweler. The box was older though, made of leather and shining with embedded jewels.

I could feel the energy shift in the room, and I twisted my fingers nervously, putting down the letter. *This* was the slight change I'd felt in the past two days.

There was an intensity between us that hadn't been there before. It felt like there were obsidian threads of magic pulling me forward, urging me to lean into his touch. I'd always felt the need to be near him, but before I turned eighteen it had been far more subtle. I had no idea what to do with that though, and I couldn't ask him if he felt the same.

I was almost positive that he didn't feel the same.

I knew that dragons eventually found fated mates, and I knew that wouldn't be me for Gage. If I was, wouldn't he have said something? That would be obvious, right?

Plus, I wasn't a female dragon, and while the dragon population wasn't extensive, there were plenty of options, most likely. Yet Gage had never dated anyone, at least not that I was aware of. But he also had never acted like *that* towards me, so I didn't want to bring up my own feelings.

When he did find someone in the future, I didn't want him to ever doubt that I was anything but happy for him. And I would be. I would be heartbroken but happy for him because it would mean so much future joy in his life.

I swallowed down those emotions as he motioned me over, then gently placed the box between our two hands and met my gaze.

"I had it specially made. It was supposed to arrive two days ago, but it's here now," he murmured. "I can't wait to see it on you."

Feeling a string of excitement, I took the box from him and opened it. I felt my heart almost stutter to a stop. *Holy...* Holy fates. I swallowed and tried to sort through my emotions. This wasn't the first time Gage had gotten me jewelry—in fact, it was one of his favorite things to do—but this?

This was something else.

The thin silver bracelet was embedded with diamonds, and the two sides met to form a dragon with obsidian-colored scales, bronze eyes, and gold wings. It was absolute perfection.

"It's gorgeous," I whispered, my eyes brimming with tears. "I don't know what to say."

"Give me your wrist." He motioned as he removed the bracelet from the case and wrapped it around me. Instantly, I felt a warm, almost honey-like feeling go over my skin. I inhaled sharply as emotion crowded me, and I realized that it fit *perfectly,* like no other jewelry had before, and not just size-wise. It almost seemed to tighten against my skin until it felt molded there.

"Beautiful," he whispered, holding my gaze.

Leaning into him, I wrapped my arms around him and tried to ignore the raging inferno of affection inside of me, demanding that I tell him how I feel...

This should be enough for me.

So why didn't it feel like it?

Chapter 3

Bexley

The following morning, I was woken up by Ms. Payne. The soft knock on my bedroom door had me letting out a small tired sound that should have come across as 'come in' but most likely made no sense. Her soft laugh filled the space as she walked into the spacious room and opened up all the large windows, flooding it with golden morning light.

Instantly I was grumbling and burying my head back under the ivory silk comforter that smelled faintly of cinnamon and whiskey. Probably because Gage had fallen asleep next to me watching movies.

"Good morning, Ms. Bex. Here is your coffee! We finally got that creamer in." She put down a silver mug etched with gold font next to my bed as I slowly pulled the covers back, eyeing it cautiously.

"The peppermint one?" I asked softly, trying to contain my excitement.

"The very one. Bet you don't want to leave for school today now," she hummed in amusement. I blinked sleepily, trying to process her statement.

My eyes went wide in panic, flipping the covers back. "What did you say?!"

She offered me a smile, setting my breakfast down on my dresser. "Didn't you read the packet? You are leaving for campus today."

"What the heck?!" I scrambled out of bed and darted past her into the living room, grabbing hold of the packet in question and kneeling down in front of the coffee table, sorting through the papers. I groaned, realizing that she was right.

August 28th. Move-in day.

"Who sends an envelope out the day before?!" I squeaked, rubbing my eyes as I looked back down at it. Ms. Payne offered me an understanding look, but I also didn't *really* feel like she felt bad for me—there was way too much mirth there.

"Don't worry, Mrs. Bronzeheart has sent staff to come to pack up your things. That was why I came to wake you up." She nodded towards the door, where three female staff members were staring at me with wide eyes.

I blushed as I grabbed a blanket on the couch and pulled it over me, feeling self-conscious about the silver silk sleep set I was wearing. I mean, I was completely covered up, but still. I wasn't even wearing a freakin' bra.

"Of course. Let me grab my coffee," I murmured and hopped up as she began giving them instructions. I easily slipped on a robe instead of the blanket, a big fuzzy white one with my name on it, and added some slippers before grabbing my coffee and allowing them to go into my bedroom to pack. I blinked, looking back at the papers, wondering why Gage hadn't mentioned us leaving today.

I mean, I was excited, but holy fates was this moving fast!

"Bex!" a feminine voice sang brightly. I turned towards the door of my suite, smiling brightly as Gage's mom brushed past Ms. Payne and pulled me into a hug. I could practically feel the excitement radiating off her as she flitted to the door of my bedroom, nodding her head at the clear progress they were making.

When she looked back at me, I noticed her chocolate brown eyes were filled with way more emotion than usual. That didn't surprise me completely—Celine Bronzeheart was one of the most authentic, warmest, and kindest individuals I'd met in my life.

When I'd first been brought here, she had instantly welcomed me, and I knew now that she was the closest thing I would ever have to a mother. I think in part she loved to have a surrogate daughter because she always complained about the house being overrun by grumbly male dragons. She wasn't wrong, to be fair. Although, I think we all knew the truth—what Celine Bronzeheart said was law.

"I know this is all extremely fast, but do you feel comfortable leaving today? We can always try to delay—"

I cut her off and shook my head, squeezing her hand. "I promise, it's totally fine. I was just taken off guard and a bit worried about packing. As long as they manage to pack at least half my clothes—"

"Half?!" Celine asked, looking alarmed but offering me a big smile. "Absolutely not! You have the wardrobe most girls would die for. I will have everything sent over, even if I have to do it myself."

"You don't have to do that," I promised, trying to hide my smile as I took a big sip of my coffee, loving how the peppermint exploded on my tongue.

"But I will anyway." She winked and then looked down at her elegant watch. "I actually just came to let you know you have about an hour until you need to leave. The car will drive both Gage and you, so if you want to get ready for the day, he should be here by the time you're done. I know he and Leo had a meeting today before he left for the year."

I nodded. "Sounds great, I'll go get ready... Is there anything I should wear, specifically?"

"It's a bit colder there, but dress like yourself, Bex." She offered me a small smile before turning more serious. "Promise me that you will be yourself. Don't let anyone there tell you that you should act differently."

I inhaled and nodded. "I promise."

Seemingly happy with that, she turned to Ms. Payne. I slipped into my bedroom, grabbing a few items before going to get ready for the day. I knew they would pack all of my cosmetics last, so I had at least a bit of time. I walked towards the side windows of the room that faced the private garden and opened them up, the small opening allowing for privacy while also letting in the comfortable morning breeze.

As I filled up the tub, I realized I could smell a faint scent of storms coming our way despite the clear skies. I'd always had a keen sense of when it was about to storm, and it fueled my love for them. I hoped that they would have some at DIA.

From what I'd learned about the school from Gage, each sector had a different weather pattern. I hoped that the shifter one was similar to the even temperatures at home. I didn't do fantastic in super cold weather.

Once the bathtub was filled up and I'd brushed my teeth, I twisted my hair up so it wouldn't get wet before slipping into the warm water and letting out a happy sigh. While sipping on my coffee, I briefly wondered if I was in way over my head with this school.

I mean, that was more than likely, which is why I was so glad that Gage would be with me. *It would be totally fine.* A bit of an adjustment, but I had never come across any shifter that hadn't been perfectly polite. Some were a bit pushy because of my connection to the Bronzehearts, but they always backed down when Gage arrived on scene. I knew that if he was with me, there wasn't so much to worry about.

I would continuously remind myself of that and hopefully end up less nervous.

I must have soaked for about twenty minutes, having already done a full spa routine yesterday in celebration of my news, before our movie night—so it was really more of a way to relax from the sudden adrenaline rush Ms. Payne's words had caused. And I felt extremely serene by the time I dried off and slipped back on my robe, walking to the mirror to look over my complexion. In the last month or so, I'd gotten a fair amount of color, and while it was never really warm enough here to lay out and tan, my time in the garden had clearly left my skin more golden than before.

It had been some time since I'd thought about how I looked.

In large part because I rarely left the estate, and when I did, I was surrounded by the Bronzehearts. But now, headed into the academy? I couldn't help but wonder if I would stand out. Every shifter I'd met had dark hair, and maybe it was just this region of the territory, but my golden waist-length hair usually caught a lot of attention. Not always the attention I wanted either.

In fact, in the past week alone when we had gone into town, there had been several times that Gage had to intervene with a few men, and women, trying to touch it...something that was both awkward and unsettling.

It wasn't just my hair that stood out, though. My build was far smaller than most shifters, and I often felt like I had to stand straighter just to compare. My golden eyes darkened with concern that these odd insecurities would only get worse around what was sure to be an entire school of gorgeous shifter females.

Females who Gage had known for at least a year...

No. I wasn't going to go there.

The two of us had an amazing summer, and I felt closer to him than ever. Plus, he'd mentioned in passing how busy he'd been at school, and I hoped that meant he hadn't found his mate or dated anyone. I wasn't positive how I would react to Gage dating, truth be told. I would of course be happy for him, or at least try to, but the concept made my stomach tighten uncomfortably to the point of sickness. It was actually painful to imagine a world where Gage was with another woman.

Sorry, not 'another' woman... He wasn't with me.

Shaking myself from those thoughts, I got dressed, deciding to go with a cute ensemble I'd yet to wear. The cream-colored suede skirt was high-waisted and cut mid-thigh with a slight flare. I tucked a loose, almost semi-transparent white blouse that tied at the neck into the skirt, paired with a white bralette underneath. I added on a glitzy bronze belt and then slid up my thigh-high transparent socks and looked over my reflection in the mirror. I smiled slightly, feeling my cheeks heat because I sort of looked...sexy. I blinked, my cheeks turning light pink, before walking towards the door, not wanting to chicken out of wearing it.

"Cupcake!" Gage's voice had me smiling as I threw open the door and nearly rammed right into him. I tilted my head up and offered a big smile to him, his eyes filled with that dark intensity that had my skin breaking out into shivers.

"Hey you," I teased, "my *supposed* best friend who

didn't even tell me that we were leaving for school today!"

He flashed me a gorgeous smile. "I didn't want you to stress," he said as he smoothed a hand over my cheek. "Now it's more like a surprise."

"A surprise?" I offered an arched brow, leaning into it.

"Were you not surprised?" He chuckled knowingly.

"I was," I murmured and then looked over at him, realizing that along with his normal attire he was wearing a dark sports coat, his family's bronze crest standing out on his chest. "Oh, fancy jacket."

"Don't worry, you have one waiting for you." He said it like he was joking, but whenever Gage mentioned having something for me, he usually meant it.

Plus, it wasn't exactly unusual for him to put his clothes on me, especially if they had the Bronzeheart crest. I think he did it to remind me that I had a safe place and a group of people that loved me, so I didn't mind it at all. Even if he didn't intend it that way, it was how it made me feel—like there was a big shield between myself and the world.

That shield's name was Gage Bronzeheart.

"Is this good to wear?" I motioned to my clothes.

I know he mentioned that we used a portal to get onto campus. It was actually the only way to get on campus and was solely responsible for why I'd never been able to visit him at school. Not that I would have had the nerve to do that, but it still had bummed me out to have to wait around to hear news of his return.

Although, it wasn't exactly like I had to wait long. Despite not being allowed to have technology on campus, like our cell phones, every night he sent me a short message about his day that I would respond to. It wasn't a lot, but the small exchange back and forth, much like my pen pal notes, had fueled the lonely months before his return on holidays and finally the summer.

Never again. Now it would just be us at DIA, every day together like normal. Our normal.

Gage's rumble that vibrated through his chest and escaped his throat had me realizing that he was looking over my outfit. "You always look perfect, Bex, but you better be wearing a coat with that, or else I will end up murdering someone."

I blinked, surprised by his words. "What?"

My confused and surprised tone seemed to snap him out of something I didn't fully understand, and he leaned forward, pressing a kiss to the top of my head. "Nothing, cupcake. Just go grab a jacket and shoes."

I nodded mutely, shocked by his words. Murder someone? For what? My clothes? That seemed a bit drastic. After all, his own mom was the one that helped me pick them out. I went to my closet, ignoring the comment for now while slipping on a warm long tan jacket and flat boots that laced up to right over my knee in ivory leather.

Once I was done, I adjusted my hair and looked back to find him staring at me despite the chaos of everyone in my room packing up. I blushed and looked down, pretending to check my shoe, before seeing the box of notes at the bottom of my closet. Crap, I couldn't leave that behind, could I?

"Gage!" Celine called. He grunted and turned towards the main room, his mom asking him something. I crouched down to grab the box and brought it over to one of my suitcases, slipping it underneath some clothes before going to grab a bag for the stuff I may need throughout today.

The cream-colored satchel was lined with sparkly fabric, and when I added a few items into it, I realized there wasn't much I needed that wasn't being packed. Hopefully I would have access to my suitcases almost right away. Still, I decided to add a hat and gloves into it, on the off chance that I did get cold before having the chance to change.

Sliding the pack onto my back, I adjusted my coat so

that my cuff would still show, and then said, "Alright! I'm ready."

I didn't look up right away, staring at the piece of jewelry I refused to take off. My favorite one I owned. Even Celine had fallen in love with it and often complimented it, going as far as to tell Mr. Bronzeheart about it.

His reaction had been a bit different as he and Gage had a small silent conversation before he had looked at me and told me it was a piece of true art.

I think that meant he liked it?

Even after all this time, Leopold Bronzeheart was a confusing man to read. I knew he was happy I lived with them, and he often told me how proud he was of me and my success with our tutor, but outside of that, we didn't interact very much. Then again, the man was busy keeping an entire clan running, so I couldn't exactly blame him for focusing his priorities.

"Do you have everything?" Gage asked, excitement dancing in his eyes, telling me that he was glad we were leaving for school. I didn't know if that was because he was excited about school or excited about going together.

I closed my eyes, running through everything I could need, before I looked towards my large armchair in realization. Normally covered in my knitting supplies, which had been packed, there were currently three plush stuffed dragons sitting there. I looked at Gage, who was leaning in the door and offering me a knowing look.

"I can't bring them," I sighed. "That would be ridiculous."

"It's not ridiculous to keep something you love close," he said honestly before offering me a gorgeous smile. "Plus, that's our family you're talking about."

I let out an unintentional laugh, nearly a snort, at his words as I went to grab them, the bronze, silver, and gold dragons all fitting into my backpack. They weren't large and could easily sit in the palm of Gage's hand, but they were special to me because each had been here waiting for me when I first arrived. The two of us jokingly called them our kids, which was ridiculous...sort of. No, it was obviously ridiculous, because I had never thought of marriage or kids.

Mostly. Not with Gage, at least.

That was a lie.

"Hey." Gage turned me so that I was looking up at him. "Are you okay?"

"Nervous." I exhaled and then closed my eyes, groaning into his chest. "You know how I am with change." When he wrapped me up, I felt all the tension drain from my body.

"I also know that you're amazing at adapting. This is

going to be a good thing, cupcake. An amazing thing," he murmured softly. I believed him.

I pulled back and nodded, the closeness of our faces surprising me as my eyes darted down to his lips unintentionally. A rumble broke from his throat, and for just a moment I thought I saw a need in his eyes, an expression that almost looked hungry... And then I heard someone laughing in the other room.

Mr. Bronzeheart.

"That would be my dad to see us out," Gage murmured.

"Well, we better get going," I teased as he led me towards the door. "Can't be late."

"There they are!" Celine grinned, standing next to Leopold, who offered both of us a warm look and hug in greeting.

The atmosphere was comfortable as they walked us through the garden towards the large circular driveway, where our luggage was being loaded into an armored SUV. I had heard a lot of people call the Bronzehearts' security measures 'extreme' or 'unneeded,' but I didn't think that was the case. I didn't know about all the threats my family faced, but I knew it had to be substantial to go to the lengths that they did to keep us safe.

I looked back towards my wing of the house, feeling weird knowing I wouldn't be back for a few months, before putting my bag in the back. Then I walked up to Gage and listened to what his father was saying with curiosity.

"Estrid is opening up the portal for each individual clan heir today; the rest of the shifters were told to arrive later for security purposes." He sighed, looking frustrated, which was an expression I wasn't used to seeing on him. "If you run into Jagger or Breaker—"

"Dad, I go to school with them." Gage chuckled, slight tension in his voice as he continued, "I can deal with them. Plus, I have Bex by my side, and she's downright terrifying."

I nodded earnestly, knowing it was far from the truth, as his father laughed and looked down at me with warm affection. "Be careful, okay? If you need anything, you know you can always come home. Both of you. The next break at school is for Autumn Harvest, but Gage will give you a cell phone to use discreetly, so if anything goes wrong—"

"We will let you know," I agreed softly before looking at Celine and then him. "Thank you guys so much, you're both amazing."

Celine threw her arms around me and hugged me tight as I heard Gage saying something about his mom not lasting the week. When I finally pulled back, she was smiling despite the tears on her cheeks, and she ushered us into the car. I slid in first, followed by Gage's large frame. I let out a sigh, sinking into the comfortable leather seats of the SUV, glad there was a divide between us and the driver.

Sometimes I worried the staff judged how comfortable I was with Gage because of who he was. It was ridiculous, but... I was still worried.

I didn't want to ever make him look bad.

"My parents love you," Gage said as we pulled away from the estate.

"I'm easy to love," I teased, bumping into his shoulder.

His eyes flashed bronze. "Yes you are, cupcake."

Chapter 4

Bexley

I knew he didn't mean them in a romantic fashion, but Gage's words stuck with me during our twenty-minute drive to the portal location. I peppered him with a few questions about school, and I loved how relaxed and at ease he seemed. Although, much like myself, when it started to storm outside, his energy levels spiked with excitement, the inside of the car becoming increasingly lively as I leaned into him.

It didn't surprise me that his magic grew more vibrant with each rumble of thunder. Unlike myself, Gage didn't just love storms, he *thrived* off of them. Literally, his magic fed on them.

In Trabea, there were hundreds of different types of shifters and even more sub-species within that. However, one of the most dominant was dragons. It wasn't based on population size like the wolf shifter packs either. No, this was because of pure and unadulterated raw strength. It was because they could pull on their own threads of magic that most other shifters didn't have access to, and it made them the most powerful and dominant species. It was why there were three ruling clans to split up Trabea, and it was why the shifters underneath each of the clan territories had to submit to their rule.

In fact, there was only one place where that wasn't the case, and it was the southern mountain range...but only rogue shifters went there. Or at least that was the rumor.

While all dragons were powerful, usually drawing on their strongest elemental affinity, being a storm dragon was considered the epitome of power. It was what all three clan heirs were, and it was what their family lines consistently flourished on for years now. It had always surprised me that none of the three families had a female heir, but I knew that wouldn't have necessarily been considered a good thing.

Male storm dragons could mate with anyone, and the heir they produced would be a storm dragon, so the families always hoped for a male heir to continue their line. I supposed once they had one, they decided to stop?

It was the only reasoning I could come up with.

Female storm dragons would produce storm dragon heirs as well, even if they didn't mate with a storm dragon, and that was extremely dangerous considering they produced in a litter, unlike other female dragons.

Apparently, the few female storm dragons that had existed were constantly hunted and under threat because there were dragons, and even other shifters, that wanted to use them to create a mass population of storm dragons to upset the power balance. Something that would be far too easy to do since their clutches were usually at least a dozen.

I nearly shook my head at that... I couldn't imagine having twelve children. Although, that didn't upset me nearly as much as someone trying to hurt female storm dragons purely for that purpose. I felt my jaw tighten, absolutely hating that concept. I just hoped that type of mentality was far in the past now.

I wasn't positive what I'd do if I found out that was still considered acceptable.

A rumble of thunder drew me from my dark thoughts as I realized Gage was trying to draw my attention. I blinked and looked up at him, my cheeks heating. "Sorry, I was thinking about storms and magic."

His eyes lit up at my words. I knew he liked it when I told him exactly what was on my mind, and it had become something of a habit. The issue? I didn't have much of a social filter. Sometimes I said things to him that I found embarrassing even though he thought they were adorable.

"I'm almost sad we're leaving today," he said as he looked out the window. "I have a feeling this would have been a fun storm to fly in."

I had seen Gage shift before. It wasn't something he was supposed to do often, but he had, and I knew from the one time I'd flown on his back that it was absolutely exhilarating.

"Hey, what's with the sad face?" He gently tugged up my chin.

"What sad face?" I offered him a bright smile and then deflated when I realized he wasn't buying it. "I don't know, Gage, I'm just nervous. I have literally zero shifter skill sets. I just have a lot of random information stuck in my head from all those long tutoring sessions. I probably just scored high enough on the written to make up for the 'I'm a shifter but can't shift' thing. I mean, I have twenty-five classmates out of thousands that took the exam... It just doesn't make sense that I got in."

"Yes it does," he growled softly. "You are brilliant, cupcake. You don't have to believe it, but it's obvious to everyone."

I put my head against his chest and took a deep

breath. I was glad he thought that, but it didn't take my insecurity away.

"You're worried about others realizing you can't shift?"

"Of course I am." I gathered myself, straightening and meeting his gaze. "There isn't anything I can do about it, but of course I'm worried. Heck, that isn't the only thing I'm worried about. I feel like my brain has been buzzing since getting that letter."

"What else are you worried about?" He encouraged me to open up, causing my chest to ache. I very much wanted to express my concern but I promised I wouldn't ask...

"I just don't know your life here, Gage," I admitted. "I don't know your friends, the classes you take, the sports you play... I don't know any of it. I don't know if you have a girlfriend—"

And it was out there.

Gage's face turned dark as his eyes deepened in color. "Girlfriend?"

I bit my bottom lip nervously before releasing it. "Yeah. Don't people date at DIA?"

"Some shifters do," he murmured, darkness filling his handsome face, "but I have a fated mate, cupcake. I would never date another woman."

And that was the reason why I would be in love

with this man forever. The loyalty he displayed towards others, even a mate he didn't know, was incredible.

I nodded, trying to shield my emotions before moving on. "As I said, I just feel like it may be a weird adjustment. I mean... Do I have roommates? I saw the information mentioned roommates." There! Look at that smooth, perfect transition that he most likely saw right through. If he did, though, he didn't call me on it.

I saw hesitation fill his gaze as he smoothed a large hand over my arm from where it was wrapped around me. "Some people have roommates."

"Will I? Do you?"

"I do not." He seemed to tense slightly, adding, "And neither do you. Well, not in the traditional sense."

"Why?" I asked in confusion.

"Because you were put in the specialty dorms for the Storm Dragon Clan heirs."

Specialty dorms...with the Storm Dragon Clan heirs?

"What?" I demanded softly, feeling my head pulse slightly. "Why? Aren't people going to be pissed? I mean, I am not a dragon and very much not an heir."

Gage stared at me for a minute and then grunted. "I don't really care if they are pissed. I'm not letting you live in some massive building with a bunch of hyped-up shifters I don't know. I'm sure as hell not letting you sleep around them. I need you close to me, Bex. There are too many unknown factors on the campus. It's a safe place, but it can be dangerous."

Oh. I felt my body relax as my head stopped hurting. My frustration at the clear change in my living conditions, orchestrated by him, melted into understanding. I knew almost everything about Gage, and if there was one thing he cared about, almost obsessively, it was my safety. I could see the determination in his gaze, and I let out a huff, pretending to be upset.

"So we are essentially roommates?" I teased.

"Technically they are separate structures," he drew out, "but yes, you will be very close by." Something told me these dorms were a true 'specialty' by the way he'd already described them.

I finally cracked a smile. "Fine... I guess I'll live with you. But I won't apologize for blasting music and dancing late at night. You had the option to get rid of me and instead chose this." And I loved that he'd chosen it.

"Your 'late' is like eight," Gage mused, "and you are usually knitting by then, already dressed for bed."

"You can't tell people that at school!" I exclaimed. "They'll think I'm lame."

"It's cute." He smiled softly. "I wear the scarf that you made me everywhere."

Oh.

I still shook my head and turned fully into him with a serious expression. "While I absolutely love that, no telling people about that. What eighteen-year-old goes to bed by eight and knits? Seriously, Gage."

"You. So a perfect one." He flashed me a charming smile. "Also, it's too late. Your knitting skills are going to be known campus-wide once I tell everyone that you made my favorite scarf. I get compliments on it all the time."

Well, that boosted my ego, to say the least.

"Gage." I narrowed my eyes. "Don't you dare."

"Oh, I'm going to dare."

Before I could convince him otherwise, the car came to a stop, and the teasing mood slipped into something else as I looked out towards where the rain had lightened to a drizzle. Convenient. I also had a feeling that it was magically altered because I could practically feel the charged sensation in the air as Gage opened the door.

I felt nerves and exhilaration slam into me as I stepped out and looked over the lush grassy hill in front of us. I tightened my hold on my bag as I heard him say something to the driver about luggage.

I wasn't focused on that though.

No, I was focused on the gorgeous hand-carved wooden arch that stood proudly at the top of the hill. I approached it, noticing that the base of it was covered in vines and plant life. Trees stood on either side of it, and the intricate carvings, I realized, showcased different types of shifters, from rabbits to dragons.

It was so unique and beautiful that I nearly reached out to touch it, stopping myself as Gage approached from behind.

"Amazing, isn't it?" he asked, wrapping a hand around my hip and stopping me from moving forward. I nodded mutely. It was more than amazing; it was a piece of art.

Before anything else could be said, electric energy seemed to fill the space, something that had been a small buzz turning into a sensation I could feel under my skin. I stepped back further into my dragon as the empty air beneath the arch became silvery in material and swirled in a hypnotic pattern.

That wasn't even the most shocking part.

No, that was when a beautiful, serene-looking woman stepped out of the portal, looking polished in her immaculate suit and pin-straight blonde hair. Her blue eyes met mine as a friendly smile filled her lips, then she slowly turned her attention over my head.

"Gage Bronzeheart, good to see you," she greeted. "And you must be Bexley."

"You can call me Bex," I offered and put out my hand. "It's wonderful to meet you."

"Headmistress Estrid." She met my hand. "I have been looking forward to meeting you as well. What a unique situation you have gotten yourself into, first living on the Bronzeheart estate and now in a specialty dorm."

I frowned slightly, her words striking me as odd. She sincerely meant that she found it unique, I could tell that, but it also felt like she knew something I didn't. I mean, I suppose that was to be expected since she was the headmistress.

"It was something we cleared," Gage explained, not sounding concerned exactly, but a bit tense.

Estrid's gaze jumped with humor as she addressed him. "I'm aware, dear boy. And you should be aware that you are the first heir arriving at campus. The others haven't come through the portal yet."

"Good." He tightened his grip on me. "I wanted to show her around before it got too crowded anyway."

Estrid looked down at me and smiled again before motioning to the portal. "Feel free to step right through. Bex, I sincerely hope I see you again."

I nodded, feeling much the same.

I did, however, feel like I was potentially missing something. There was an undertone to their conversation that I didn't fully understand. Before I could ask though, Gage intertwined our fingers and walked us right through a portal for the first time ever in my life.

* * *

I'd never experienced a portal before, so I didn't know what to expect...but I quickly learned. The blast of magic that went over my skin had set my entire chest ablaze, and I felt nearly out of breath, glad to be wrapped in Gage's arms. It wasn't until we stepped out of the portal that I realized my eyes had been squeezed shut, and my entire body was hot as if I was about to break out into a sweat.

I heard Gage swear before he cupped my face and spoke softly. "Bex, relax, cupcake. You're shaking."

Was I? My eyes flew open, and almost like I had ice water thrown over me, everything cooled in an instant. I stared into his bronze eyes until my breathing regulated, and I realized I had absolutely no idea how long we'd been standing there.

"That was intense," I whispered.

Intense was only one way to describe the insanity of traversing into different sections of our plane of existence within seconds. I gripped onto Gage, feeling a bit unsteady as he looked over my face, then the rest of me, as if checking if I was injured in any way. Luckily, the odd burning sensation was disappearing, and all I was left with was feeling a bit embarrassed for my extreme reaction to going through a portal.

"Are you okay? Do you need to sit down?" His voice was a soft, warm rumble.

"I'm okay," I promised. "I just hadn't expected that... It felt like less than a second, but I could also tell we were traveling. My skin got so hot." I felt breathless after my ramble, and my lips pressed into a small smile as I felt an exhilarating energy go through me. "That was... insane. That was so insane."

Gage's eyes sparked. "If you liked that, just wait until you see everything that's waiting for you in the sector. This place is nothing like home."

My gaze followed his own towards the five gates to the right of us. I stepped away from him for a moment and looked around the pavilion, finding myself curious about where we had landed ourselves.

The space was circular in nature, the arch behind us still glowing as if Estrid would join us any moment. She didn't though, and my gaze moved down to the stone surface beneath my boots, which was beautifully laid with a skill set that was reflected in the massive three-story academy building that it led up towards. Doors stood open, and I could see students milling about, all of them seemingly perfectly at home and comfortable here.

"What's that?" I asked curiously.

"Administration building," he explained as we walked forward, the temperate climate running over my skin. I realized that there was no wind or anything else; it was just completely neutral. "This is where the headmistress works, as well as counselors. We need to pick up your packet and then we can head into the sector and to your dorm."

"Our dorm," I corrected, and he flashed me a smile.

I stopped suddenly and looked to the right, where there were large walls and five gates that guarded their secrets so well you couldn't see anything past them.

"Those are the sector gates?"

"Yes." He wrapped a hand around my waist, his thumb doing small circles on my skin. "Shifters, witches, demigods, fae, and vampires."

Of course I knew those other species existed, but I couldn't imagine interacting with others that weren't shifters. I felt a small curious urge to go check them out but figured I would start small and maybe work my way up to meet others outside of our sector. After all, it wasn't like I interacted with many people outside of our estate.

Turning my attention to the left, I noticed there was a lone gate standing there. "What's that one?"

"Demons," Gage rumbled, and then encouraged me to walk forward. "I promise to explain everything more, but let's get your papers. I want to get you into the sector and safe in our dorm. I didn't consider how worked up I would get with the idea of so many students around you."

"Even though they are all the way over there in the building?" I pointed out curiously before adding, "And you mean your dragon?"

His eyes flashed bronze. "Yes, even with them all the way over there."

He didn't answer my other question, and I didn't push it as we walked up the large steps and entered the building. It felt good to be under his arm, even more so to imagine he was the one worked up instead of his dragon, and I was so caught up in his scent that I didn't even realize that the entire space had gone silent as he led me towards the correct table. It was clear that everyone in here was shifters right now... So why were they staring? Specifically at us?

I stumbled, blushing bright red at my clumsiness as Gage caught me against him and let out a defensive snarl that had eyes snapping down respectfully around us.

My skin broke out in a shiver at that. Why did I like that so much? It wasn't like Gage used that tone at home, but something about the commanding nature of it really set my entire body on fire.

"We are here to pick up her packet," Gage said evenly as we approached the table. All three students, two males and one female, were staring between the two of us in absolute shock. I leaned further into him, their gazes moving to the lack of space between us.

I started to shrink, feeling extremely uncomfortable. Why were they acting like this?

"Packet. Now."

They scrambled as I stared up at Gage in interest and a bit of confusion, never having heard such a sharp demand in his tone. Was he upset? When I met his gaze, it was filled with affection, and he pressed a kiss to the top of my head, making me relax. Okay, not mad. At least not mad at me.

When a packet was handed my way, I grabbed it from one of the men. My coat shifted slightly and my bracelet shone underneath the comfortable lighting. I couldn't help but appreciate how sparkly it looked underneath these lights.

"Holy shit."

I jolted at the other male's voice as Gage let out an actual growl, turning me away from them and leading me back outside. I could hear quick talking and nervous chatter behind us, but I was far too confused to look back and try to see what they were saying.

"What was that?" I asked in confusion.

He cursed and then exhaled. "I'm sorry, Bex. People are idiots, especially around any of the heirs. I promise you won't have to deal with much more of that...hopefully."

"I don't understand what they were upset about."

"They weren't upset, just shocked," he explained, leading me towards the gate. "Not only have I never touched a woman here—"

Oh man, that made me way too happy.

"—but I have made it very clear you're under my protection, which to most shifters is a huge deal despite being our normal."

Our normal.

I smiled at him as we approached the gate. "I like being under your protection."

His rumble made me smile as he gripped the handle of the large gate and pushed into it, the creak sounding through the pavilion. I could feel magic run across my skin as we stepped through into what almost felt like a misted cloud.

I tightened my grip on him as we walked past the cloud into what could only be described as a gorgeous forest paradise. I came to a full stop on the path underneath us, looking around in wonder. Gorgeous dark stone buildings with wood accents and large windows littered the landscape, some larger than others, as a soft cool wind, just like back home, brushed through the space.

Emotion hit me square in the chest as I looked up at Gage. "We are *really* here."

"Together," he agreed.

Holy fates. This was insane.

Chapter 5

Gage Bronzeheart

"This is spectacular."

Bexley's hushed whisper brought my attention to her plush lips as she stood at a complete stop, looking ahead with wide eyes. I could see the awe in her expression, and I was momentarily mesmerized, as I was with most expressions on her face, because she fascinated me so much.

It was like looking at a piece of priceless art that you knew you couldn't touch... But I did. I touched her all the time. It was the purest, sweetest form of torture, and I planned on continuously subjecting myself to it.

I was never letting Bexley go. She'd been trapped in my estate for this long, stolen from where I'd found her, and nothing would change now that she was with me at

DIA. She was absolutely mine, and eventually I would show her that... Just not yet.

A frustrated groan nearly broke from my throat at that thought. Everything felt like a goddamn waiting game when it came to my cupcake, and I wanted nothing more than for it to end. I wanted nothing more than for her to understand everything.

"What's wrong?" Bex asked sweetly as I looked down, realizing that my hold on her was tight, staring at her lips. The woman always dressed like a goddamn cupcake, and today was no different. I craved to unwrap her, to taste her as a treat for how patient I'd been.

"Wrong?" I rumbled. Nothing was wrong because she was here and in my arms. Although, I would much rather be tasting her lips. I couldn't though... Not until she understood what was going on here. Completely. I swallowed down the familiar guilt, hating that I was keeping secrets from her.

They weren't secrets I wanted to keep.

Fates, I would love nothing more than to tell her everything—her past and our future. Because there would be a future, no doubt about it. But I couldn't. Which was why my parents had sent her here in the first place, despite it being possibly dangerous. We needed a way for her to break out from under the spell that held her hostage. We needed a way for her to remember what and who she was.

Until then, there was absolutely nothing I could do, because even oblique mentions of her past caused her unbearable pain... So I would wait. If any place could be responsible for unleashing the magic inside of you, it was Dark Imaginarium Academy.

I looked forward to that day because it was also the day I could claim Bexley, knowing that she was fully aware of what that meant.

"You're rumbling." She offered me an amused look before stepping forward, turning to walk backward while taking in the lush autumnal landscape that surrounded us on all sides. I tracked her movement, not wanting her to slip away from me. I also was a tad worried she would trip. I wouldn't say my cupcake was clumsy...but sometimes the ground seemed to be distinctly against her.

"It's my dragon," I excused easily.

It wasn't a lie, it just was also not the full truth. My dragon was a part of me, literally half of my being. There was no separation though, and while that primal side of me became more prominent at times, it was still me.

It was me when I stole Bexley's things and added them to my 'collection.'

It was me when I purchased the beautiful jewels that I loved covering her in.

It was me when I pinned her against the wall because I didn't trust myself with her desire scenting the space.

It was always me. But it made it far easier for me to explain by saying it was my dragon.

As I said to Bexley, I would never cheat on my fated mate, and since I hadn't told her I'd met my mate... Well, I didn't want her to think I was like that. I'd been so fucking confused when she'd mentioned the 'girlfriend' thing in the car. Didn't she realize I worshiped the ground she graced?

"I know," she admitted, a hint of sadness filling her gaze before she turned back around, leading me down the wide path that led into the shifter sector of the academy. It was a unique space, and Bexley stood out like a diamond.

The entire sector was based on the forested landscape around it, and unlike our estate back home, the campus had a very relaxed feel to it. In part because it was created to be a perfect place for shifters, allowing them to enter the buildings in their shifted or non-shifted forms, with large open doorways and landing spaces even on the higher floors. Not that I ever shifted on campus if I could help it. It drew far more attention than I wanted.

No, the only attention I wanted was that of the gorgeous blonde in front of me, and luckily, she seemed to want to give me that...and more. I just couldn't take her yet. I couldn't take what she was offering so sweetly, even when she didn't realize it. I always protected Bexley—it was my fated duty—and I wouldn't start our lives together when she had a significant gap in her knowledge.

I just needed to be patient... Something I was capable of.

My two friends that she would soon be meeting? Well, I had a feeling it would be a bit more difficult for them. I knew they were resentful that I spent every day with Bexley, but that would change now. Despite what I told Bexley, everything would change, and I was praying to the fates that we would figure something out soon before I broke my promise.

"What are these?" She stopped right at the entrance of the campus. On either side of her were two large structures that almost looked tent-like in nature. They were made of dark timber with full glass fronts, the walls coming in at a peak to make a triangle. The entire campus was surrounded by forest regions, so they matched for sure despite their unusual shape.

"They are used for 'general curriculum' classes. You'll find your schedule in the packet," I explained easily, placing a hand on her slim back. I felt my cock twitch at the memory of her sheer little top and that damn skirt. I was thankful she was wearing a jacket now because I wasn't positive I could handle it if not.

"I really need to look at those," she murmured softly.

"We have all day," I promised her, not wanting her to stress. "You will probably have around six classes per semester, and each run about once, maybe twice a week."

And the rest of the time she would be with me. I was already struggling with the concept of her not being at my side...or worse, in a class with males.

Yeah, that was going to be a problem.

"Less than tutoring," she teased with amusement, causing my own smile to form. Something that was a constant around her despite not being my normal here at school. Bexley wasn't wrong, though—one of our tutors had left quite the impression on both of us. Thankfully he'd retired, but there had been a solid two years when we were forced to spend twelve hours a day buried in books.

I had no doubt my father had arranged for that purposefully to keep us out of trouble. Something that was directed towards me far more than sweet Bex. No, I knew I was the problematic one here. I was the one who was constantly fantasizing about pinning my best friend against the floor and taking her like a fucking animal.

It didn't help that I knew she found me attractive. Something that was constantly tugging at my control, begging me to give into the primal urges associated with Bexley being my mate. Surprisingly, that wasn't my largest issue though.

No, my darkest thought, my biggest fear, was that my cupcake would never remember everything. That I would never be able to claim her as my mate and make her mine. That she would never feel the emotional intensity that I felt for her. At least I couldn't assume she did before feeling this bond... Hell, I couldn't trust myself if I ever found out that she did.

I could barely handle that she found me physically attractive. The many times that she'd told me she loved me, even though she didn't mean it the way I craved for her to, I'd nearly lost my shit.

The things I wanted to do to Bex were not okay—*I* was not okay. I was fucked up over her.

She came to a stop suddenly, turning towards me with wide eyes as I intertwined my fingers with hers and cupped her jaw with my other hand. "What's wrong?"

"So the general curriculum classes are for everyone...but what about the specific shifter classes? I don't have an animal type. Even if I was put with freakin' bunny shifters, Gage, I wouldn't do well. I have no idea what it's like to be a bunny!"

Her words were rambling and adorable. I wanted desperately to kiss her mouth shut, to tell her everything that would remove those thoughts, those insecurities, but I couldn't. Not without hurting her.

"I promise you that everything will be fine, cupcake," I murmured. After a moment, she nodded and broke away from me, back to her normal level of energy. My gaze caught the glint of her cuff under the sunlight, and a surge of pride slammed into me. I wasn't supposed to mark her, I knew that, yet I'd had a custom cuff made for her, and one that didn't symbolize just *my* connection to her.

My father had known what it was and hadn't tried to stop me. He knew the time for not doing anything was coming to an end. She was eighteen, and I needed to find a way to fix this situation because I wouldn't be able to control that other side of myself forever. The side of me that demanded all of her. That craved her in a way that couldn't be healthy.

"What are those?" she asked suddenly, bringing my thoughts back to the present.

Looking around, I tried to view the campus through her eyes, the picturesque autumnal landscape featuring two large, long buildings that were log cabin-like in nature and directly across from one another on either side of us. In front of us was an enormous stone building that had doors that were large enough to easily allow my dragon through. That wasn't what she was looking at though.

No, she was focused on the small circular buildings scattered throughout the area that looked like cylinders with wood around the top of it as a roof as well as at the base. Inside there was room for around five people at most.

"The pods are smaller teaching classrooms or meeting spaces, the large long buildings are dorms, and then the main one is where most of the classes are held as well as the dining hall," I explained casually before offering her a smile. "Pretty easy setup, so you can't get your cute ass lost."

Her cheeks flushed a pretty pink that I could guarantee traveled down the rest of her perfect body. "Did you just call my butt cute?"

I wouldn't use cute exactly, but I did like her ass a lot. I'd imagined bending her over constantly... Then again, I loved every single part of Bexley, so that shouldn't have been surprising.

Before I could answer, someone called my name. I snapped my head up and narrowed my eyes, wrapping an arm around Bexley and drawing her further into me. I knew what it would mean to everyone on campus, with me putting such a large claim on her, and I was more than proud to do so. I would just have to make sure people kept away from her until I could figure everything out.

Until then, I would need to scare off assholes like this.

"Walker." My voice was hard as Bex rubbed her cheek against my shirt, almost subconsciously trying to squirm closer to me. I nearly groaned at the feel of her ass against me, unable to hide how hard I was. If she noticed, she didn't act like it. Instead of running from my arms, she pressed closer.

"I was wondering when you would show up." His words were completely unsurprising to me.

Walker was the beta to one of the future wolf alphas here on campus, one of the most prominent families, and he was always trying to cause fucking problems. I watched as he caught Bexley's bright orange scent, stopping fully and moving his gaze down to her small frame tucked into my arms.

I didn't try to stop the growl that emerged from my throat at that point. He shouldn't be looking at her, let alone be anywhere near her, especially close enough to smell her scent. The fact that it was faintly twisted with desire in an intoxicating combination only made me that much more possessive.

"What do you need?" I demanded, wondering if it would make Bex upset if I moved her behind me. But when Walker's eyes moved down her body, I'd had enough. I stepped in front of her with a vicious growl leaving my chest.

"Eyes off her. Now."

Walker jolted and paled upon seeing my expression, seeming to snap out of the daze he'd been in. I understood the effect my cupcake had on others, but I didn't have to like it, and a fucker like this needed to keep his gaze to himself.

"Right. Of course. You know what, I think we can just talk later."

Bex's hand slid up my back, trying to soothe me as I offered him a dark look.

Walker scrambled to leave, clearly understanding my patience was absent, as I brought Bex back around into my arms. I led her towards the main building in front of us, wanting to put some distance between us and Walker. I knew if he had the opportunity, he would go out of his way to start shit, and I wasn't okay with that in the least. I was just thankful I was with her right now.

The idea of him talking to her when I wasn't here had me nearly fuming—

"Gage!" Bex squeaked as I looked down and blinked, realizing that I had her pinned against the stone wall of the building. *Fuck.* I swallowed, not knowing how to explain, and my immediate reaction was to step back and distance myself.

But I didn't.

Instead, I lifted my fingers up and brushed them against her jaw, knowing I needed to apologize despite my reaction being completely normal for the situation. She didn't know that though, and I was acting far differently than usual. Yet instead of letting her go, I continued to stare at her.

The late morning sun highlighted every gorgeous freckle on her skin, and while I preferred storms, the light always made my cupcake look like a goddess. I knew what she looked like at all times of the day, from the early morning to right before bed, and I wanted to experience that every day for the rest of my life.

"Sorry, cupcake," I apologized.

"Sorry?" she asked in confusion, as if trying to pull herself out of the strong connection between us.

"I didn't..." I looked between us and then swore, hating how much I loved this. Why couldn't I have more control? Why couldn't I keep my shit together? Bexley deserved more than this.

Instead, I was savoring the feeling of having my mate captured and pressed against me. Enjoying the primal concept of having caught her, which made her absolutely mine—as if she wasn't already. I just wished I could truly make her mine.

"You didn't mean to pin me to a wall?" she asked softly, her cheeks pink.

I had, though. Even if I hadn't actively made the choice, I had.

"I don't like males around you," I admitted softly. Her eyes turned liquid, like melted gold, and surprise filtered in. "Especially ones like Walker."

"Why?" It was a valid question.

"I don't trust him," I explained, "but more than that, I can tell he wants you."

"He wants me?" she parroted, looking confused.

I knew that she didn't believe me, at least not fully.

The estate had been a safe haven for Bex, and she rarely had to deal with men like Walker—which good, because I would have probably killed someone if not. Growing up as a teenager, barely able to control my thoughts and emotions, paired with being a dragon? And around a woman I was obsessed with? It had been a lot.

There were a few times I'd nearly been sent away by my own father.

"Yes," I confirmed.

"And that bothers you?" I noticed that her eyes were starting to bleed black from the center, creating a beautiful mixture that I knew had to do with her magic. A magic I desperately wanted to see unleashed.

I didn't answer her. I wanted to so badly, and I could see it in her eyes as well. She wanted some confirmation about this bond between us. I couldn't though, so instead I said, "If he ever tries to talk to you and I'm not around, you have to tell me, okay?"

I saw the slight disappointment in her eyes, probably because I hadn't said more, but she nodded as I kissed her forehead gently, holding her close. One day I would explain it and explain why I was concerned. Bexley was gorgeous, there was no doubt about it, but more than that, there was something about her that drew people in like a moth to a flame. I could practically feel the desire other males felt for her, and she would never recognize it, which put her in danger.

There was a softness to Bexley that I wanted to keep, a light that hadn't been tainted by others, and while I knew I couldn't keep her sheltered like I always had... I didn't want men like Walker around her.

He wasn't worthy of her.

"Want to see your dorm?" I asked curiously.

"The special one?" She wiggled her brows as I pulled away, chuckling softly and intertwining our hands before leading her around the large building. She watched me with interest as we reached the back and came to the stone-laid path that curved through the thick forest trees ahead.

"Your dorm is back here?"

"We have a separate path and section," I explained as I led her towards our destination.

It was maybe a minute walk, if not less, when the path narrowed as if petering out, before expanding out into a massive clearing. I stopped at the edge of the tree line and let her eyes move up towards the impressive structure we would be living in. One that had been constructed very purposefully.

"This is it," I announced as her lips popped open.

It was difficult to describe our dorms—if you could call them that.

Rather, they were four houses on large iron columns at least five stories up in the air. Their dark wood exteriors contrasted the bright skies and the bridges that connected the three large houses formed a triangle around the center building, a set of secondary bridges leading to the center. The bridges were small, sturdy walkways with railings, and despite being perfectly safe, would allow for the illusion of being up in the air.

Something I knew Bexley would love.

"These are so unique," she whispered before offering me a concerned look. "But how am I supposed to get up there?"

I grinned, loving the spark of excitement I could see bubbling within her. I nodded towards the large columns underneath each one. "Each of them has elevator access in case we want to get up or down that way instead of shifting. That is my preferred way."

"You don't like shifting?" she asked, looking confused.

I loved shifting. Absolutely loved it.

But what I didn't love was the extreme control I had to maintain while shifting so that I didn't find a way to break out of campus to find Bexley and claim her. My dragon didn't see nearly as many issues with the current situation at hand as I did.

"Wait." She tilted her head. "Who else lives here? I thought it was just us?"

I led her forward, trying to keep my smile subdued because Jagger and Breaker would lose it if they heard the hope in her voice at living alone. It wasn't her fault that she wasn't excited at the prospect of others being there—as far as she was aware, she didn't know them.

"Remember my father mentioned Jagger and Breaker?" I reminded her.

Her cheeks flushed at their names as she stilled, seeming to have a moment of confusion, as her fingers came up to her temple in a telltale sign of a headache. Fuck. I hoped this wouldn't be a problem when it came to them, but I knew how sensitive the spell made her. I tried to figure out a way to soothe that.

"They live here as well, all the Storm Dragon heirs do," I explained as she looked up at me.

"Have I met them before?" She frowned. I knew everything was telling her that she had—that she knew who they were—but that instinct was covered. Buried.

"Until school started, I hadn't seen them in some time," I hedged, not directly lying to her.

"So probably not," she filled in where she thought I was going with it. "So is that normal? For them to place three shifters like you all together?"

"No," I admitted. "There's a reason there is only one Alpha of each clan, and putting three future ones inside the same dorm, even with separate living spaces, is asking for trouble."

Although, considering our past and the future at stake, it wasn't a problem at all. In fact, despite not being siblings and our families preventing us from hanging out with one another, the two of them were the closest thing I would have to brothers.

"So why?" She examined the structure again as we reached a large metal door.

"I have a feeling they think it shows unity and that it's easier for security purposes since we are so high profile." It was for those reasons and so many more.

"That must make blending in hard," she murmured. I knew she had been uncomfortable with the amount of attention on her already, and I didn't know how to ease that besides serving as her shield every step of the way.

"Unfortunately, that's not an option here," I said as we stepped into the small elegant foyer and I pressed the button for the elevator. I led her into the small space, and when the doors closed, I used my large hands to turn her into me and scanned her face, noticing the tension and anxiety displayed.

"What's wrong?" I asked.

"I'm just worried how others will view me," she admitted. "I mean, it's one thing to live with someone that is considered so elite, but once they realize I can't shift? I don't know, Gage... Maybe it's better for me to live with the other students. I don't want to cause any unnecessary—"

"No," I immediately growled out, causing her to jolt. I tried to soften my words, as the elevator came to a stop.

"You have lived with me for this entire time. That's not stopping now."

Before she could respond, the door opened and she turned to the house we arrived in, a sound of happiness coming from her throat as I smiled.

I may have made sure that this was a place Bexley would never want to leave...

Chapter 6

Bexley

I would never be able to live anywhere else—that much was clear.

Holy fates. When I stepped out of the elevator and looked around at the large room, I was taken off guard by how perfect it was. No, seriously, like very specifically perfect to my tastes.

The living area was bathed in sunlight from the back window, which arched up into the roof, allowing for almost a greenhouse effect. It would be the perfect place to watch storms, and in the center of it was a pair of french doors that led to a balcony, which wrapped around the entire structure. Each of the other houses had wrap-around balconies as well, and they were all connected to each other and to my dorm in the center by thin walkways. It was such a unique setup, and as I looked around the space, moving away from Gage, I felt excitement string through me.

I knew he was responsible for how beautiful this place was. The school may have been the one to build the structures, but the cozy living space that featured a small modern kitchen, a large fireplace, and a series of comfortable surfaces to curl up on, was completely Gage. He'd even put some of my favorite throw blankets in here, the velvety material tempting me to lay down.

Despite being small, the space felt luxurious, and I found myself trailing my fingers over the cream-colored velvet couch. Tilting my head, I noticed that there were lights hanging from the ceiling so that even at night there would be a warm glow to the space.

Somehow, those weren't even the best parts... No, the part that got me was the view. I walked forward to the set of french doors and opened them, looking out over the forested region that expanded out behind our dorm. I also took the opportunity to peek at the other houses, and I couldn't help but wonder who had claimed each one.

Despite feeling a bit unsure about having two room-mates I didn't know, something about their names alone felt comfortable. It didn't feel threatening or intimidating. Sure, I would no doubt feel a bit shy, but more than anything I felt excited.

Turning around, I noticed that Gage was lighting a fire, and it drew my attention to two doors, one on either side of the fireplace. I crossed the room after putting down my bag and opened the first door, finding a sizable, gorgeous bathroom. The floors were made of white marble that seemed to sparkle under the chandelier lighting, and the clawfoot tub in the center of the room took my full attention despite the gorgeous shower, vanity, and mirror.

Baths were a not-so-secret pleasure of mine, and I'd been convinced that I would have to stop taking them here. Luckily, that seemed far from the case.

"This is your suite," Gage explained, appearing behind me in the door. "Your bedroom is through the other door."

"This is beautiful. Seriously Gage, I don't think academy dorms are supposed to be this luxurious," I expressed softly. "Fates, I'm not complaining, I just didn't expect this."

Gage approached me and pressed a kiss to my nose. "Only the best."

Damn him.

I swallowed nervously as a question popped into my head. "Does everyone come here to use the kitchen? Not that I mind, I just want to know what I should be prepared for."

His eyes lit up with amusement. "After dinner I'll show you my suite. Each has a kitchen set, exit, as well as a living space. It is a smaller-scale version of this. Although I will still be here most of the time unless you plan on coming by my place. You can't get rid of me that easily, cupcake."

I blushed. "I never said I wanted to get rid of you." Rather the opposite.

His smile was gorgeous as he cupped my jaw. "Just remember that setup so if the other two use it as an excuse to come in here, you'll know they are lying."

"Would they do that?" Once again, I felt a weird excitement surge through me at meeting them.

Gage's expression turned serious, and he looked deep in thought momentarily before offering me a small smile. "I think they may do a lot I wouldn't expect."

Okay...

"Are you guys friends?" I asked hesitantly.

This was the part that I was still somewhat unsure about, the dynamics of Gage's life here. I knew that we were each other's best friends back home, but what if I had to share him with someone here? What if he had another best friend?

"Yes," he immediately answered and then ran a hand through his hair. "It's a bit more complicated than that though. Before our families cut peace ties with one another, we were friends."

"Because the clans don't trust one another," I murmured, remembering that from one of our many tutoring lessons.

"And we hope to change that." His gaze held something heavy before offering me a small smile. "Go check out your bedroom, cupcake. Then I want to make sure you eat. You didn't have breakfast."

I nodded, deciding not to ask any more questions for now, wanting to meet them myself. I also found it somewhat amazing that Gage paid attention to small details like that about me. I knew the man had a million other things on his mind, but he took time to check if I had breakfast or not. Following his directive, I slipped past him and went to the other door, loving the crackling of the fireplace that filled the space.

When I opened the door, my breath rushed out of me...because *wow*.

The room featured a massive circular bed in the center of it, the pale pink and gold bedding making it look like a nest. I had to fight the urge to go to it as I noticed the carpet on the ground was white faux fur with sparkles that matched the subtle shine of the sheer curtains that went fully around the room.

They didn't stop the light from coming in through

the large glass panel that, much like the main room, stretched along the back and up on the ceiling, a pair of french doors leading out to the balcony and walkways. It was both cozy and light, relaxed lighting hanging from the ceiling in small lanterns. When I turned around, I realized my suitcases were lined up against the closet wall that was shared with the bathroom. I was very much ready to get settled, and if it wasn't for knowing that Gage would insist on food, I would stop to do so. There was something so relaxing about organizing your stuff when you've finally found a place you wanted to stay, whether that was a home or vacation.

Despite having been here only minutes, something about this room felt *right*. It felt like a home I could end up loving.

"This is something else. It's like something out of a fairytale." I exhaled and turned back to find the man watching me with an intensity that almost seared me.

I froze, my breath catching as he walked close to me and smoothed his hand under my jaw, tilting it up as he examined my expression.

"Ready to go get something to eat?" he asked, making me blink and pull back slightly. *Food.* He just wanted to go get food.

Fates, Bexley—he wants to eat food, not you!

So why did I feel like there was something else

growing between us? The same thing I'd felt since my birthday. Something I wanted to understand but was afraid to look into too much. I knew if I was misinterpreting all of this, I would be disappointed.

"Yes, of course," I agreed happily.

As he led me back through the house, I thought I saw something soaring through the sky, but before I had a chance to get a good look, we were stepping back into the elevator. I inhaled, leaning into my best friend as my brain went a bit hazy with the comfort of being around him. Luckily, I managed to keep my desire tucked away, slowly learning how to control it despite it always being there towards him.

I had a feeling that would never go away.

I felt my head pulse slightly as a memory came to me, the test day pulling to the front of my brain in startling detail as I remembered one other time when I'd felt an almost uncontrollable reaction towards someone...

I was done. I couldn't take the test again, and I'd done my best. I gripped the counter of the bathroom I'd snuck into and put my head down, letting out a relieved breath. I'd been so nervous, but after three days of intensive testing, it was done.

There was nothing more I could do, and there was some relief in that, in it being over, no matter the result.

Nodding to myself, I turned and walked back out into the hallway outside of the testing hall we'd been in. The space was now nearly empty as everyone crowded into the halls. I caught the scent of so many different shifter types, and looking over the faces of everyone present, I realized that it wasn't just potential first-years here.

No, there were older students here for the summer, or maybe for the end of the school year, who had yet to go home? I was glad Gage was coming home and hadn't decided to stay here. Which reminded me... Where was he? He said he'd wait for me.

I went up on my toes, looking around before grabbing the strap of my bag on my shoulder tighter, and trying to move through the crowd. Eventually, I realized I wasn't making progress because of how small I was compared to many of these shifters, so I kept to the edges of the hallway, not wanting to garner any attention. Someone shouted loudly, and I swallowed nervously, feeling uncomfortable.

I normally considered myself outgoing, but I was a bit overwhelmed, and this was a far different atmosphere than the Bronzeheart estate.

Unfortunately, my need to get out of here was so

extreme that I didn't realize I was on a collision course until I hit right into a large muscular back, stumbling back in surprise. I felt a weird surge of magic go over me, burning my skin, and my breath caught, making me wonder what type of shifter would have caused that reaction. I frowned, looking down at my arm, which was almost shaking with weird energy....

Then a smooth, dangerous voice had me stilling.

"Watch where you're going." The voice was commanding, and I lifted my head up, meeting a pair of unreal eyes, an icy blue that was surrounded by silver.

I was rooted to the spot, unable to look at anything else, focus on anything else, but his gaze. I felt like my fight or flight response was not only activated but in complete contrast to my actions.

I watched as surprise flashed over his face before almost panic slipped in there, his hand tightening on my arm where he had stabilized me. My head pulsed. I knew I had never met this man before, but there was something about him that seemed so familiar. This time, my head thrummed so hard that I let out a sound of pain that snapped me out of it.

"Sorry!" I squeaked, desperately needing to get away from him because all I could focus on was the familiarity I felt... So I turned on my heel and ran. I heard him say something, but I ignored it, slipping past three groups before finally seeing Gage.

I ran right into his arms and exhaled, hoping like hell that man wouldn't remember me knocking into him. He was not only intimidating, but struck me as someone you didn't want an enemy of.

"Cupcake." Gage's kiss to my ear had me looking up at him, making me realize I'd been caught in my thoughts for so long we were nearly back at the main building and the end of the forested path. I blinked in surprise and shook myself from the effects that the memory left on my body. There was something about the man that called to me, but I didn't understand it, and whenever I tried to think it through, it caused me pain.

Too much pain to force it.

"What were you just thinking about?" Gage asked softly.

"About the test to get in and the day I finished," I responded honestly.

"You were so nervous," Gage mused, "And look—no reason to worry at all."

I didn't want to disagree with him, but I had a feeling there was plenty of reason to disagree. I was almost positive that despite getting in, I didn't fully belong here. Mainly because I still couldn't shift.

Actually, it wasn't that I couldn't shift—at least not just that—it was the lack of connection I had with my animal counterpart. It was like no one was home inside of me, and it was a void that hurt more than anything.

Maybe... Maybe Dark Imaginarium Academy would be the place that helped me find that side of myself.

Chapter 7

Bexley

My stomach made a sudden noise, causing my cheeks to flush as Gage quickened our pace, pulling me from my thoughts. I let out a small giggle at how concerned he was as we entered into a large foyer featuring a timber ceiling with a gorgeous chandelier hanging from it, looped with greenery. There were a few students milling about, but I wasn't super focused on them when there was so much else to stare at. Like the enormous pair of blue doors that stood open at the entrance of the dining hall, the wood embedded with what looked like natural cut gems. It was both gorgeous and felt a bit out of place compared to how comfortable everything else seemed to be.

In fact, the more students I saw, the more I realized that I stood out a bit as well.

Everyone else was dressed far more casually than me, and I felt a sting of insecurity before pushing it away, knowing that Mrs. Bronzeheart wouldn't have led me astray. If she thought my clothes were the right choice, then I had no doubt they were. Plus, if we were being honest, I loved all my clothes a bit too much to ever significantly change how I dressed.

"This is the dining hall?" I asked in awe. I had been in ballrooms before, and that was exactly what this was despite being disguised as something different. The long tables spread throughout the room were decorated with fine dining plates and glasses, and at the front was a long buffet of food that seemed to feature literally everything there was to eat, if my nose was correct about the scents we were being exposed to. This was no doubt going to take a bit to get used to—there was just so much at once to pay attention to.

"Yep." He nodded. "Every meal is served here, and most events are held here as well."

I looked around, seeing easily how the place could be transformed into an event venue. When we reached a small table near the front of the room but off to the side, he pulled out a chair for me.

"I'm going to get you food, sit tight." His lips grazed my head as I sat down and curled up on the seat, having absolutely no doubt that he would get me something delicious. The minute he left, I turned my attention to the large windows, trying to distract myself from the onslaught of eyes I could feel directed towards us. Hopefully that was something that would calm down, because I wasn't positive I would actually ever get used to it.

It honestly was an aspect of all of this I hadn't considered. At the estate, I'd been so comfortable; I knew everyone there. This was an entirely new game with rules I didn't know and players I'd never met.

I was comfortable sitting there, relaxing from the insanity today had brought, finally coming down from the high of this brand new experience...

But then something changed.

Something, or someone, turned the air combustible. My entire body tensed, feeling a surge of adrenaline, desire, and slight fear ignite in my chest. I turned my head slowly as I shifted in my seat, trying to see the cause for my body's intense reaction, and met the direct gaze of the man from the test. The man I'd just been thinking about stood at the entrance to the room as if he'd been summoned from the fates themselves.

Oh. Wow.

If I'd thought he was intimidating before, it was nothing compared to now, and my breathing stilted as his entire body went rigid, completely freezing in place, wherever he'd been going no longer important. I felt my pulse pick up, and my face flushed as a dark heated look crossed his expression, the intensity causing me to stand up nervously, my chair nearly falling over.

This connection was so much more than what I'd even felt the day of the test. It was like those obsidian threads of mine were reaching out to him, begging for his attention. I stepped back as his eyes snapped down to my feet—

My back hit the dining hall wall as he appeared in front of me, consuming all of my space at once as the scent of peppermint filled the air, causing my skin to prickle with pleasure.

I let my head fall back as I truly looked at the man now holding me captive against the wall, then forcibly pulled my gaze from him despite it being nearly impossible. I tried to calm my breathing, but that was difficult as I found myself not only consumed by his intensity but beyond attracted to him.

The man was so large, nearly as big as Gage, and made of lean, cut muscles that his dark long sleeve shirt molded to, the material pushed up and exposing his forearms. My eyes moved along his platinum watch in appreciation, and I fought the urge to run my fingers along the piece as well as his corded muscular forearms. That would be weird...right?

Holy fates, this man was something else. As I looked

back up to meet his icy eyes, I noted frustration, almost anger, in his gaze, as well as a palpable heat that felt like it was searing my skin in pleasure. Did this man realize how beautiful he was?

His icy skin was marked in contrast with a rune on the left side of his jaw that matched the earring on the same side. His silver hair that was streaked with black only seemed to further intensify the darkness that surrounded him, and I got the impression that the man was very dualistic in nature. He had all the control in the world and absolutely no restraint at the same time. It was beyond intoxicating, and I found myself so incredibly fascinated with him.

"Hi."

His eyes widened as they fell down to my lips before traveling back up. "Hi?"

The man's voice hit me like a semi-truck, a feeling of déjà vu and familiarity rolling over me as my head pulsed. I winced, running my fingers over my temple, the man watching the action with concern that made me feel a bit...unsure? I didn't really understand my reaction to this man at all.

I tucked a piece of hair behind my ear and tried to not breathe in his scent, not knowing how to handle this situation. This man was about as different from Gage as one could get...except for maybe the intensity and the very obvious fact that he was a dragon. I didn't know how I knew that, but I did. The magic that rolled off him had me almost feeling hazy, drugged, and euphoric, and I could almost guarantee that he didn't realize it.

"What else would you like me to say?" I murmured my question, tucking both of my hands against my chest in both a defensive and reactive move. He watched the movement before his hand shot out and gripped my wrist, his fingers skimming my arm as a surprised gasp left my throat.

A wave of desire so strong my knees nearly broke had me gripping onto him, everything turning into sharp points of heat around me. He easily supported me, tugging me against him. I couldn't see or hear for a moment, his touch consuming me as my heart began a rapid, dangerous beat that felt uncontrollable, untamable. The haziness of his spell threatened to shift back over me, and I wasn't positive which I preferred.

"Are you okay?" he asked, his voice now rough, a one-eighty turn from how he'd been acting before.

"Yes." I swallowed, looking up at him, as I realized that he had the faint glint of a diamond in his right brow. I reached up and smoothed my finger over it, letting out a happy sound as he seemed to squeeze me tighter.

"That is beautiful," I admitted and then found his gaze again, which was on my extended hand—namely, my bracelet. He gently took my hand, as I stayed against him but straightened myself slightly, his eyes running over the piece with interest and what I almost thought was vulnerability before holding my gaze.

"Who gave you this?" His low rumble caused me to feel that heat of need brush through me, but I also was a bit hesitant, feeling like this man's temperament was all over the place. Or maybe I was the one all over the place...

"I did." Gage's deep, commanding voice instantly had me relaxing, but I didn't look away from the fascinating dragon holding me. I did notice that unlike usual, especially considering some unknown male was holding me, Gage seemed oddly calm. Well, maybe not calm, although I wasn't looking at his face—but he hadn't ripped me away from him yet. Normally I would want that, but right now? I liked him holding me.

The man looked over at Gage, shifting us slightly so I wasn't pressed against the wall but still held firmly against his chest, as I heard the soft *tink* of two plates being set down on the table. My stomach threatened to rumble, feeling that pang of hunger from not having breakfast, but I couldn't leave his arms. In fact, it was the last thing I wanted to do.

"Gage," the man said in greeting. "You didn't tell me when you would be arriving."

"I assumed you would figure it out." Gage sounded amused more than anything as he rounded the table, coming up behind me so I was pressed between the two of them. The man's hands smoothed over my shoulders as I observed the way he was meeting Gage's gaze, a silent conversation passing between the two of them.

"I hate when people do that," I openly admitted, drawing both of their attention. "The whole silent conversation thing. I want to be part of that."

Like I said, not much of a social filter.

Gage chuckled softly. "Come on, Bex. Let's get some lunch."

"Okay." Reluctantly, I tried to step out of the man's arms, but he held tight. Finally, when he let go after staring at me for a heated moment, I said something that seemed to surprise him. "Did you know you smell like peppermint? It's wonderful."

The man blinked at me with wide eyes as I sat down at the table, where a large plate of food was laid out.

"We need to talk—"

My stomach interrupted the man's words, and I blushed. *What?* It wasn't my fault! I had a big appetite, and if I missed a meal, my stomach was not happy about it. His look of frustration turned to panic as he sat down next to me on the other side, keeping his gaze glued to me.

"What?" I felt insecure with him staring at me. "Why are you looking at me like that? My stomach gets really unhappy when I miss a meal. That's not my fault."

Gage chuckled softly because we'd had extensive conversations about this exact thing.

"You didn't feed her?" he demanded of Gage. I shook my head, knowing that Gage would get defensive about his words, as I took a bite of mashed potatoes. I wouldn't lie, I was already eyeing the cupcake that was sitting on a separate plate, so much so that I didn't initially realize they were doing one of those silent conversations again.

I smiled, knowing it would work in my favor as I slid my hand forward to grab the—

"Nope." Gage slid the plate away as I let out a small growl of annoyance.

Our new friend's brows nearly shot to his hairline. "Did you just growl?"

I blinked, and my cheeks tinted pink as Gage hummed in amusement. "She's very territorial about food, and she will almost always eat cupcakes. It would be her entire diet if someone didn't make sure she ate normal food."

Because normal food didn't taste as good as cupcakes.

I'd tried to make that argument, but it never worked.

"Whatever," I mumbled, slicing up a bit of steak and putting it in my mouth, happily surprised by how good the food was. Wasn't food supposed to be bad at school? I thought that was a thing people said. Then again, DIA wasn't exactly a normal school.

"Oh!" I looked back as Gage started eating to find the man staring at me in a perplexed way. "What's your name? I'm Bexley. Please don't call me that though. I prefer—"

"Bex."

"Yes, actually," I said, taken aback. "How did you know?"

Pain flashed through his gaze, but it was gone almost instantly as he offered a casual shrug. "Just guessed."

I nodded in understanding before he continued, "My name is Jagger Silvershade."

"Oh! You're one of the other heirs. Totally explains your power level." And his disastrous effect on me.

I felt a small smile tilt my lips, warmth going through me as something settled in my chest at knowing his identity. My small headache seemed to slip away as I stopped searching for why he seemed familiar. His magic was similar to Gage's, and while I didn't recognize his name personally, that would be the reason for the familiarity.

I also realized now that I knew his last name. "You're from the Flicker clan. I've heard about your family."

He assessed my expression before nodding, his eyes slowly moving towards Gage like he didn't want to look away from me. "Has she been by the dorm?"

"Took her there first. I assume you just arrived?" Gage asked. "Breaker wasn't there yet either."

"I don't think he's gotten to campus yet." Jagger exhaled and ran a hand through his hair, his gaze moving towards my wrist. "Interesting choice."

"Do you like it?" I asked sincerely, having polished off half my plate. My stomach felt full, so I let out a small yawn and sat back, examining the cuff in question.

"It's beautiful," he murmured. "Quite the statement."

"A statement that I think is necessary." Gage met his gaze and held it.

Jagger looked back towards me and offered what I think was a heated look before he nodded. "Yeah, I don't disagree with that."

I looked back at my bracelet, wondering what type of statement they were talking about. Because it had a dragon on it? Because Gage had given it to me? Before I could ask, a series of loud voices caught my attention, and I realized that the dining hall was getting more crowded.

"Let's get her out of here," Jagger grunted.

"Agreed."

Despite knowing it was probably because Gage could tell others were looking at me, which I'd probably made obvious bothered me, a small part of me wondered... Maybe they didn't want to be seen with me.

That couldn't be the case though, right?

Chapter 8

Bexley

When we got back to the dorms, Jagger disappeared. I suppose it didn't surprise me—not exactly—but it did hurt my feelings... Which was ridiculous, right? Why did that hurt my feelings? I barely knew the man. I stood frozen as he strode out the balcony door, and I tried to not deflate, Gage wrapping his arm around my waist as if knowing. I just prayed he didn't ask about it since I had no reason at all to feel this way.

"Want to see my dorm?"

Immediately my excitement was back up, causing me to smile as I followed Gage towards the french doors, which opened easily to let in the cool, soft wind. I shrugged off my jacket and left it on the balcony railing, walking ahead of Gage as he let out a low rumble that had me looking back at him. His gaze was partly bronze as he offered me a heated expression that had my toes curling before motioning with his chin towards the walkway to the left.

It was an exhilarating feeling, being up high, and I wanted to slow down and look around. But I kept moving ahead, my fingers running over the safety railings as I finally reached the balcony of Gage's place. My eyes widened, seeing that he was, in fact, right—it was extremely similar. Stepping through the balcony door, I noticed the fire was going, and the style of his furniture was comfortable and masculine, like in his bedroom at home. His kitchen had less counter space than my own, and instead of having two doors, he just had one that I suspected was the bathroom. What really caught my eye though? In the back of the space was his massive bed that looked like a freakin' dream.

I glanced at Gage, who stood in the french doors offering me an amused look, then looked back at the bed. I zipped across the room so fast, not giving him a chance to stop me, and face-planted right into the soft surface.

I groaned in relief, my body half-draped on the bed with my legs, still covered in my boots, hanging off. I inhaled his scent, trying to not be obvious about it, as I let my frame sink into the luxurious sheets. I was positive my own bed was just as comfortable, but I particularly loved Gage's, even back at home.

When his shadow came over me, I expected him to hoist me up by the waist, but instead his hands came down on either side of me. I shivered slightly as his lips came across my ear. "I'm starting to think that skirt you're wearing is a horrible idea."

A prickle of heat rolled up my spine as I tried to not arch back into him, but I did push up slightly. "Why is that?"

Suddenly, his large hand came up the back of my leg and brushed over my thigh-high socks, a growl breaking from his throat. My breathing hitched, and I found myself wondering if this was him or his dragon. I didn't want to take advantage of Gage if his dragon was being difficult...

Yet I found myself arching back up to him as he seemed to press closer, seemingly worried I would try to get up, his nose brushing underneath my ear and against my neck. A whimper caught in my throat as something long and hard pressed right against my butt, my eyes widening in the realization that Gage was hard. Like, really hard. I may not have had extensive knowledge about intimacy, my tutors barely skimming over it, but I knew he was aroused, and there was a flash of pride that went through me that I'd brought that out of him.

Even if it was mostly his dragon side. I mean, it was a natural reaction to a female shifter being bent over a bed... And I was seeing the problem here.

"Gage," I whispered, "I know this is probably your dragon..."

His entire body tensed as his other hand slid up my thigh to my waist, holding me in place, his heartbeat loud and fast as he brought his lips against my ear again. "And what if it's not? What if this isn't something I can blame on my dragon, cupcake?"

Oh, fates.

My fingers curled into the sheets tighter as his one hand snuck out and grasped my chin lightly, tilting it back so he could wrap his fingers around my throat in a firm grip. My center tightened and pulsed, causing wetness to form between my thighs as blatant need, so strong it had me trembling, slammed through me.

"You don't mean that," I murmured, not allowing myself to go there.

Apparently, my words upset him because, in the flash of a second, I was flipped and laid out in the center of the bed with him over me, his large frame between my legs. I looked up at Gage's face and realized that it was him...at least partly. His green eyes swirled with bronze as they took in my body from above, his eyes tracing the way my skirt had pushed up to my waist, revealing pale gold panties.

I couldn't help the way my cheeks flushed at that.

"Fuck." He swallowed, blinking as if trying to snap out of it while his jaw tightened. It was clear, though, that seeing me like this caused him to realize exactly what was going on. Was it because I was facing him? The concept of me—looking at me, more specifically—being the thing to kill his desire, left me feeling heartbroken. It was a strong enough emotion that I knew this was the moment to pull it back.

"As I said, this isn't you," I whispered as his fingers smoothed over my skirt, seemingly deep in thought. "I don't want you to regret anything, Gage. As you said, with your mate—"

"I would never regret anything with you." He sat back and let out a rough exhale, my gaze moving down where he was still very hard. A small flash of relief hit me, realizing that maybe it wasn't completely just an instinctual reaction to a female shifter being bent over... Maybe it was about me.

"I need to get out of here for a minute." He ran a hand over his face and stepped back, his gaze moving over me on the bed. "And you're wrong, cupcake. This is me."

I watched as he strode out of the house, and I let out

a small groan of confusion, laying back on the bed in defeat. What did I even do with that?!

Nothing. I did nothing.

After laying there until my breathing calmed, which felt like hours later despite being only minutes, I sat up, having to admit to myself that he wasn't coming back. At least not right now. I wasn't positive how I felt about that. My throat tightened as I straightened myself up, feeling a bit disheveled. I left through his doors and closed them gently, unlacing my shoes and making my way across the bridge with my boots in hand. I murmured a song under my breath, trying to not over-think what had happened, as I briefly noticed a storm rolling in from the distance.

At least that was a positive.

When I reached my own dorm, I paused, looking to Jagger's place to the right. His doors were closed, and it was quiet—he was clearly busy with something, so I just went into my dorm. For the first time all day—heck, most of my life—I felt anxious... I felt alone. My eyes moved to the thick packet on the coffee table, and knew I needed to go through it. I hadn't unpacked, and I didn't even know my schedule for tomorrow.

I just hadn't expected to do it on my own.

With a small frown, wanting to put it off for a bit more, I walked into my bedroom and got to work putting away my clothes, making sure to hang them according to what I'd actually wear instead of using the color system I had at home. When I finally filled the closet, I looked down at the box in my hand. I went to the bed and sat on it, opening the lid up and looking over the notes I had with my pen pal.

Did they realize I was gone yet? Would they miss talking to me? I wish I'd known we were leaving today. I would have left a note, I would have said...something. I didn't know what, but it felt wrong just disappearing. I nibbled my lip and picked one of the notes up, not bothering to keep them in order.

You looked beautiful today, mo chuisle.
    How did the exam go?

My cheeks flushed, remembering how taken off guard I'd been when he called me 'beautiful.' I didn't know what his nickname meant, but the syllables were sweet when I sounded them out. My chest squeezed uncomfortably, wondering if I would ever get to write to my pen pal again or if they would assume I was done. I didn't like the idea of them thinking I'd abandoned them, that I'd given up on whatever it was between us.

Or maybe they wouldn't care. I suppose that was possible.

When the door opened to my dorm, I walked towards it and put my head out, curious if Gage was back. Okay, maybe, not curious—more like hopeful. Instead I found Jagger standing in the space and looking around. When he met my gaze, I saw a flare of surprise, before he exhaled. "You're here."

"Did you expect me to be somewhere else?" I teased.

"No, just not used to—"

"Me. You're not used to me being here," I offered. "I know this is probably weird."

"I don't mind, really," he promised, almost looking unsure of what to do as his hands went into his pockets in what seemed to be a nervous habit. Why would he be nervous? If anyone should be nervous, it was me—I was the one talking to a gorgeous dragon. "I just wanted to make sure you were settling in okay."

"Just finished putting away my clothes," I explained, walking back into my bedroom. "I have a few more things, and then I need to go through my packet. I would love the company if you want to hang out."

"Hang out?" He said the words as if they were foreign, coming to stand in the doorway while looking around my bedroom.

"Or not," I murmured, packing up my notes.

I squeaked as he appeared next to me, and I looked up, finding him watching me in fascination. "I would love to hang out, Bex."

Man, this guy gave me a bit of whiplash... I mean, I loved it, but still.

"Cool." I tried to not show how happy I was.

His gaze moved down to the box that was still open. "What are those?"

"Notes from my pen pal." I frowned slightly. "You're actually the only one who knows about them. I've never told Gage... I'm honestly not sure why. It seems silly."

He picked a note up and then examined the handwriting, his eyes darting outside. I followed his gaze to see where he was staring out in thought, seemingly at the third house.

"What?" I asked curiously.

"Nothing." He shook himself and handed it back. I packed up the notes as he sat on the edge of the bed, and I placed the box right at the base of my closet, safely tucked away. When I straightened, a wave of dizziness hit me, and my knees nearly broke, feeling black spots dot my vision.

Jagger caught me against his chest as he made a concerned noise. "You okay?"

"Yeah." I nodded hesitantly, feeling a bit off balance. "I don't know what that was..."

Honestly, while I hadn't admitted it to Gage or the Bronzehearts, I'd been feeling a bit off since my birthday. I'd been randomly getting dizzy, along with surges of heat that seemed to crawl underneath my skin. Of course, there were the headaches associated with certain thought patterns, but everything seemed more...intense.

"Sit down," he ordered. I nodded and went to do just that. "What do you need? Water?" he asked, sounding panicked.

"Maybe in a minute. Can you hand me that bag?"

He nodded, and I let out a happy sigh as I took out all three of my dragon stuffies and put them on my bed, smiling happily.

"What are those?" Jagger asked, his voice rough with emotion I didn't understand.

I looked up at him, blushing slightly. "I know it probably seems ridiculous that I brought them to campus, but I have had them since arriving at the Bronzeheart estate."

He eyed them and looked back at my face, his jaw clenching as he nodded sharply. "It's not ridiculous, it's perfect."

"Sometimes Gage and I will joke about them being our kids."

Seriously, Bex? I rolled my eyes and shook my head. It sounded way more silly when I said it out loud to a stranger than it did between Gage and me.

Jagger's eyes went darker as a rumble escaped his throat. "Why do you think he's joking?"

I looked back at the stuffed animals before offering him a perplexed look. "Because they are stuffed animals?"

Jagger stared at me for a moment longer before he cleared his throat and nodded. "I'm going to get you some water, need anything else?"

"Just my packet. I'll come with." I stood, and when I walked back into the main room, I realized that my knitting stuff was all in a basket near the fireplace. I loved it. I probably would have knit right now to relax, but I had a feeling Jagger already thought I was a bit weird... No need to add to it, right?

"So why do you live with the Bronzehearts?" Jagger asked cautiously as he put down a glass of water and picked up my packet, running his fingers over it.

"The truth?" He nodded immediately. "They found me in an alleyway."

"An alleyway?" he choked out.

I nodded hesitantly. "I don't remember anything before that—"

"Nothing?"

I met his gaze, seeing something I didn't fully under-stand there...like expectation. I frowned, trying to think back on that night and offer him something, but my head began to pulse. I shook it, and his eyes filled with disap-pointment.

"It's just blank, and whenever I think too hard about it, my head hurts so much," I murmured, pressing my fingers to my temples.

"Have the Bronzehearts explained why?"

His question perplexed me as I tilted my head in thought. "Because of post-traumatic stress. At least, that is what they believe."

I saw frustration flare in his eyes.

"Bullshit," he hissed, "It's because of—"

Whatever words he said next sounded like they were under water, a blast of pain jolting my entire frame and causing me to cry out as I seized up. I felt hard arms wrap around me, but the splitting headache was enough to pull me instantaneously into the dark.

Chapter 9

Bexley

"Bex, I need you to wake up."

I let out a small groan, curling into the warm, firm surface I was pressed against, not willing to give up my hold on the comfortable darkness. I didn't want my head to hurt anymore. I finally felt good, and I worried if I woke up, it would happen again.

"Please, Bexley?" The voice was filled with pain and so much concern it had me worrying about the speaker.

"I'm waking up," I murmured as I forced my eyes open to find myself cradled against Jagger, pure panic and fear on his face as he tightened his hold on me. "What's going on?"

"You passed out." His jaw tightened. "My words must have brought on... Well, they must have triggered your post-traumatic stress." His expression was censored, and I heard almost a lie in his voice.

"Didn't you say you thought it was something else?" I wondered softly. I could've sworn he'd been about to tell me something important... What did he know?

"Not anymore." He brushed his lips against my forehead. "I'm sorry, little treasure. I would never intentionally hurt you."

Little treasure? I loved that.

I turned so that I was straddling him, a bit surprised by my action but needing him to know I didn't blame him.

I spoke honestly, cupping his jaw in my smaller hands and looking up at him. "It has happened before. It's not your fault, and I would never blame you for that. Plus, I already feel better. My head doesn't even hurt anymore."

Jagger's gaze moved over my face, searching for the truth, before he explained, "You were out for about fifteen minutes. *Fifteen minutes.*"

I figured now was not the time to explain that was rather short following an incident like that, and I found it both confusing and flattering that he was so worried about me.

Shifting myself to fall to the side of him, curled up on the couch but no longer straddling him, I noticed his hands tightened into fists as if wanting to reach out. More surprisingly, I found that I wanted him to. I didn't know how to respond to his concern for me, and more so, I knew I needed to distract myself from the attraction this man was inspiring in me. I'd learned my lesson with Gage today, and I didn't want to cause any more problems.

"Are you still up for going through the packet?"

See! School was a fantastic distraction.

Jagger's face was void of emotion for a minute before he leaned closer to me, brushing a piece of hair from my face. "You're okay? You just snap back like that?"

"Nothing else to do," I reasoned and then looked down at the packet, which I grabbed. "Plus, I am more nervous about classes tomorrow than my little fainting spells."

"Little fainting spells?" His voice was almost choked.

I nodded, wanting to push past the moment. "I am hoping this packet isn't nearly as intimidating as it appears."

After a moment of staring at me, he nodded slowly, as if accepting it was time to move on.

"The packet?" He took it from me and looked it over. "I promise it's not intimidating. It's actually a lot of bullshit, tons of rules that don't apply to you, so the main thing you need is the class schedule."

He pulled out several thick piles of paper and retrieved a single sheet, tossing the rest down, his brow furrowed as I followed his gaze to the paper. I wanted to ask him about the rule thing, but I felt like it could wait for now.

"Your general curriculum courses make sense: *DIA Introduction & Basics, Hierarchy in Shifter Dominance, History of Trabea*, and then *Shifting with Ease...*" His voice was so smooth and calming that the things he said were tinted with easy comfort and a lack of stress. He was making it seem like this would be no big deal at all, despite one of my classes directly contradicting the tiny little problem of me not being able to shift at all, let alone with ease!

He continued, "But these other two... You have been put with bottom-level shifters for your *Understanding & Communicating with Your Animal Counterpart* and *Handling Animalistic Urges* courses."

"Seems about right. They probably don't know where to place me since I've never shifted."

Jagger examined my face. "Do...do you know what your animal is?"

"Never felt a connection to it, so no," I whispered, trying not to be embarrassed. "I know everyone is going to assume I got into DIA because of the Bronzehearts. I mean, that makes sense, doesn't it? Even if I did well on the written portion, I'm still a shifter who can't shift. I'm almost positive that it places me on the bottom rung of the bottom-level."

Jagger turned his body further towards me and spoke softly, the conversation caught between the two of us. "Even if you haven't shifted, even if you haven't met your animal...that doesn't take away from the fact that you are *not* weak. In any way. That's very obvious."

His words were not only sweet, but I could tell he meant them. I had a feeling that this man seemed far more intimidating than he actually was—I would bet he was secretly super sweet all the time.

I offered him a small smile. "Thanks, Jagger."

The hard footsteps on my balcony had me looking over to where Gage now stood, holding several bags of food that smelled delicious. I had to admit though, considering the look he was giving me, I didn't feel particularly hungry. Was he mad at me? He looked at Jagger, frozen in the doorway, as I realized that we probably looked rather close, curled up on the couch as we were. I didn't move though.

There was a small part of me that hoped he was surprised by the two of us sitting together. I knew it wasn't right of me, I knew that... But I also found myself far more hurt about the situation earlier, now that I was looking at him. I also was feeling embarrassed.

"I brought back dinner," Gage offered, walking towards the kitchen. "I'm assuming you're joining us?"

I knew he was talking to Jagger, who let out a hum of agreement, but I could feel his eyes were focused on my expression.

"I am going to run to my room real quick," I murmured, standing up and slipping away from both of them...or at least trying to. I let out a surprised sound as Gage's hard arm wrapped around my center, catching me at the door of my room as he brought his lips to my ear.

"I'm sorry, cupcake. I shouldn't have walked out." His voice was filled with a true apology as I relaxed into him and nodded. He let me go then, and I slipped into my bedroom, shutting the door and wondering what would have happened if he hadn't left. I knew I shouldn't have let my thoughts go there, but they did.

I could hear the two of them talking as I decided to get changed for the evening, knowing I needed to not be alone right now. I was already overthinking every-thing—maybe being around them would keep me distracted to an extent. I slipped on a pair of silky light blue lounge pants and a bralette that matched, tying a light knit wrap sweater around my waist. I put on my slippers before walking back out...right into an argument.

"I told you to be careful," Gage clipped at him, making me wonder if he had told him about my condition as well, before looking me over with concern. "Why didn't you tell me you passed out?"

I blinked and looked between the two of them, noting that Jagger looked pissed. "You weren't here, and when you did get back, you put the food down while I went to change. There wasn't exactly a lot of time."

I tried to not shy away from his tone, but I didn't like it at all. I'd never known Gage to lose his cool, but that's what it seemed like was happening right now. His eyes were shifting with bronze, and his magic seemed to be flooding the space with a dark energy I wasn't used to.

Gage, as if sensing my dislike, exhaled, running a hand through his hair. "Sorry. I didn't mean to sound like I'm pissed, but you have to tell me stuff like that, cupcake, okay?"

I nodded. "I know, Gage. It was an accident. Jagger didn't mean to do it."

"Bullshit," Gage hissed, glaring at our roommate.

I looked to Jagger, who was watching me with guilt. "I'm going to go..."

"No!" I was in front of him, not understanding what I was doing fully but trusting my instincts. "I don't like that. I don't like that you two keep walking out...Well, not *keep* walking out, but have walked out. It makes me feel uncomfortable and sad. Please don't."

Jagger's face filled with surprise and maybe a bit of vulnerability before he admitted, "I just wanted to get you a blanket so you didn't get cold. You barely have anything on."

"Oh," I whispered, feeling stupid. "Never mind then."

"No, not 'never mind,' I will make sure to not storm out." He pressed a kiss to my forehead and walked through the doors. I turned back to Gage, who was directly in my space, completely overwhelming it while cupping my jaw with a frown marring his expression. I knew he could tell I was upset, and it was mainly because he could feel, like myself, that something was off between the two of us.

"I'm sorry, Bex. I'm on edge today. It's not an excuse, but you know I don't normally act like this." His forehead pressed to my own as I inhaled his scent.

"It's okay, Gage," I promised softly.

"It's not, but I'll make it up to you." He brushed my nose and stepped back. "Jagger wasn't a piece of shit while I was gone?"

"No. Besides the entire passing out thing, I showed him my stuffed animal family and then we went through the packet... *What?*" Gage was chuckling suddenly, finding something about my statement beyond amusing.

"Did you say it was our family?" he asked.

"Well yeah, but I told him I was joking," I said, avoiding his gaze..

"Hey, don't let them hear that." He nodded towards the door while unpacking the food from the bags.

I cracked a smile at that and leaned against the counter, playing with the ties on my sweater as my mood turned a bit more serious. "I also told him about not being able to shift. He noticed they put me in lower-level shifter classes for my non-general curriculum courses."

Gage stopped putting away food and walked towards me, running a hand along my jaw that I leaned into. "Never be ashamed of that, okay? Do not let anyone, ever, make you feel ashamed for something that will naturally happen when it's meant to."

"That's easy for you to say," I whispered, my eyes stinging as the emotions of the day hit me. "It's embarrassing, especially because I live with three high-powered shifters. Like, there is very clearly something that doesn't fit here...and it's me."

"You fit. You fit perfectly," Jagger's voice rang out, making me look up to where he had slipped in silently.

"Don't let any of the shifters here make you think differently."

Everyone kept saying that. I knew they didn't mean it as a warning, or I didn't think they did, but I was starting to wonder just how these other students would react to me.

"Would they? Try, I mean?" I hedged. I figured I would face some backlash, but I wanted his honest opinion. Sometimes I worried that Gage sugar-coated stuff for me.

"Yes," Jagger said, ignoring Gage's frustrated groan. "People here are assholes, especially the wolves."

"Which brings me to an important point—there are some people you should be careful of." Gage led me towards the couch and I sat down, his large frame crouching in front of me. Jagger went over to the food and began taking stuff out.

"Like individuals or..."

"A few of those, but mainly groups—for all intents and purposes, you are going to be considered in the same circle as the three of us," Gage explained. "Of course, you are under my protection—"

"Ours."

Gage shot Jagger a look, my heart squeezing happily, but he continued, "Ours. But that also means you gain our enemies."

"Enemies?"

"Yes, and friends," Gage conceded. "There are only a few main players that are important to watch out for, but on the off chance one of us is not with you, you need to know who to look out for."

"There are shifters from all over, and some of them have clan representation. Those individuals, no matter what type of shifter you are, are friendly," Jagger added while bringing over a plate of food for me. I offered him a sweet smile and began to nibble on the light snack of cheese, crackers, and grapes.

"The ones you need to watch out for are the individuals coming from the city where the clans don't rule, where there are smaller packs. I can point them out to you tomorrow, but it is a fair bet that you can avoid most wolves. They have made a point of avoiding any clan territory," Gage rumbled, looking pissed.

"Assholes, all of them," Jagger agreed, watching me with a softness as he nodded towards the plate. I kept eating, loving that he prompted me to do that. I had no reason for loving it, but I did. Plus, I was *never* going to say no to food. I think that was the only part of my shifter side that I did experience—a dragon shifter-level hunger.

"And then the bears," Gage said on a sigh. "We have

a bit better relationship with them, but it isn't good by any stretch of the imagination."

"Okay. Wolves and bears—bad." I nodded.

"Then there are the water shifters, a tiny group that has banded together to constantly remind people or try to remind people of how dangerous they can be out of the water," Gage continued, exhaustion flashing over his face. "You will face the most hate from them because they feel like they are constantly being ignored."

"Are they being ignored?" I asked, wanting to understand.

"All clans rule differently." Jagger ran a hand through his hair, looking upset about his own words. "They aren't treated the best, and it's something that needs to be changed, but it shouldn't be brought here. Not into the academy."

"This sounds like a lot of people to worry about," I admitted.

"You shouldn't come in contact with most of them," Gage assured. "But if you do, like I said, you need to tell me."

Jagger pinched the bridge of his nose, clearly irritated, but didn't correct him. I knew he was also including Jagger, even if he didn't say it... What about Breaker though? What part did he play in this dynamic?

Honestly, it felt odd to not have met the man yet. It

was like he was meant to be here, and I had no idea where that notion was coming from outside of him being a roommate. While Gage and Jagger, surprisingly, were protective over me, that didn't mean he would be the same... So why was I including him?

"Okay." I looked back down at my food, suddenly not hungry. "Honestly, I'm a bit nervous about tomorrow. I feel like it may be a bit overwhelming."

"It will be."

Jagger's answer made me nibble my lip as Gage shot him a look. I let out a small sigh and nodded, standing up and walking towards my bedroom with the envelope. Closing my eyes, I fell face-first on the bed and just laid there, letting the mattress support my weight completely. It was a silly way to handle it, but it made me feel better as I left the envelope and climbed up into the center of the plush surface, deciding to take a nap. I had only wanted it to be a short nap, maybe thirty minutes, but my body seemed to disagree. I didn't wake until hours later.

Jolting, I sat up with a start, pushing my hair out of my face and looking around, realizing someone had tucked the blankets around me. Moonlight shone down and into my room, and I looked up at it, realizing the skies were particularly clear. For a moment I wondered if I was dreaming, because everything was so quiet and peaceful. Even back at home, I had never been in a place this still.

It made me feel...almost lonely.

I had no idea what time it was, but it had clearly been several hours. My heart was racing despite not having been woken from a dream, and the sheets twisted around me began to feel less constricting as my heart slowed. I let out an exhale and ran a hand through my hair, wishing that Gage was here.

I knew I could go to his dorm. I knew he would allow me to sleep in the same bed with him—it wouldn't be the first time—but I also knew I wouldn't be able to control my desire after today, and I didn't want to make things awkward for him.

Standing up, I wandered towards the balcony doors and opened them, stepping outside onto the platform as I tightened my sweater around me, looking to both sides. Inhaling the fresh damp air, I realized that it had rained a bit while I slept, the balcony's surface wet and cold underneath my toes. It felt good to be outside, and I stood there, feeling undecided on going to Gage's dorm...before noticing the dorm in front of me was warmly lit. I tilted my head, feeling more than curious about meeting Breaker and assuming that he was finally home.

Would it be rude to go to him? Especially assuming how late it was?

Instead of overthinking it, I walked barefoot along the walkway, letting out a soft hum, the wind carrying the sound. When I reached the door of the glowing dorm, I reached my fist up and knocked, but instead of making a sound, the door creaked open. I stood there for a moment, looking into the space as I considered calling out to him. It didn't feel right just walking in without permission.

"Hello?" I called out softly. "Breaker?"

When no one answered, I looked back to see that there was still a faint glow from my own main room, a large figure on the couch and one on the floor.

Had...had they both slept over? Even with their beds so close by? I loved that.

It also meant I could go back if I wanted, yet instead of doing that, I stepped into the room. I had already opened the door; I might as well take the risk and hope he wasn't a violent shifter.

"Breaker?" I called out again, but I didn't hear any response, nor did I see anyone. Yet despite that, a hazy, almost honey-like feeling worked over my skin as golden threads lazily reached towards me. Was that his magic? I could practically feel its potential to ignite, and I wanted to savor it, sitting down on the large armchair facing the fire and wrapping myself up with a blanket to wait. I rubbed the soft material against my cheek, realizing it smelled of vanilla.

It was wonderful.

My eyes grew heavy, a weird buzz traveling through my system. I decided to close them for just a moment, the weight of the day clearly exhausting me far more than expected. It wasn't until a rough, large hand smoothed over my cheek that my eyes flashed open.

"Oh." My breath caught as I found a gigantic man in front of me.

Frozen for just a moment, I blinked, taking him in, unable to tear my eyes away from the size of him. It almost seemed unreal. Maybe I was imagining him? He had muscles on his muscles, and that was only on his shoulders, which were highlighted by the firelight. He had to be crazy tall, because he was looking down at me despite being crouched in front of the chair. I paused, feeling momentarily dazed as I finally met his gaze, realizing that there was a wild note to the magic surrounding me.

Something that both felt familiar and foreign... His magic was different from the others', but I also wasn't surprised by it. Instead, it ran against my skin pleasurably, as if greeting me. Shivers broke out along my skin as a sound I didn't even understand escaped my throat.

"Hi?" I offered, hoping it would work better with him than it had with Jagger. When the man didn't say anything or change his expression, just continuing to look over my face, I realized it probably hadn't been the right move. But because he wasn't saying anything, I didn't know what else to do besides look right back.

His blonde hair was messy and wild around his gorgeous face, and I could see that despite not wearing a shirt, he was wearing pants. My cheeks flamed as I thought of how I would have reacted if that hadn't been the case. In the faint firelight, I couldn't see much more of him, but I did notice there was a scar on his jaw, and it only seemed to bring my attention to his two different colored eyes. One was so dark it was nearly black, and the other, the one not affected by the firelight, was pure metallic gold.

I should have been scared—this man was beyond intimidating—but instead all I could focus on was the hazy satisfaction of the magic he radiated. A low rumble escaped his throat, and my hand came out, resting on his chest that felt scarred to the touch. He tensed, but when I went to remove my hand, he grabbed my wrist gently and held it there.

"Why are you here, *mo chuisle?*" His voice was a deep, low vibration.

At first, I didn't realize what he was saying, but then my eyes went wide. "What did you call me?"

His eyes flashed with something I didn't understand. "Nothing."

"My name is Bex, but that nickname... I have only heard it used..." I hesitated. There was no way, right? Maybe it was a common nickname?

"Bex." He released a soft hum of satisfaction, like he enjoyed saying my name. "What are you doing here? A little shifter like you shouldn't be coming to my room at night. Especially if you belong to the other two sleeping in your dorm."

"Jagger and Gage? I mean, I don't belong to either of them..."

He chuckled softly, his voice tinged with darkness. "Now I don't believe that. Who do you belong to, Bex?"

"Myself?" Why did I sound so unsure of that?

After examining my face for a minute, he offered a small smile. "No, *mo chuisle,* I don't believe that you don't belong to anyone. And if you don't, you do now."

Oh.

"And who would I belong to now?" I asked curiously. This conversation was so intense, and yet I felt nothing but comfort. I felt like I was being roped into agreeing with something I didn't understand, and I was doing so willingly.

"Me." His words were serious and rumbled. The haziness I felt had me leaning into his touch as he brushed the hair away from my face. I snuggled into his palm and nodded as if he had asked me rather than told me. He made a pleased noise, and my eyes grew heavy as he pulled me into him.

"*Breaker*. That's your name, right?" I asked in a soft murmur.

"Yes," he confirmed, his voice filled with a depth of emotion that I hadn't imagined was possible. "I'm Breaker."

With that, I fell asleep in the arms of essentially a stranger.

Chapter 10

Breaker Firespell

Mo chuisle.

I don't think I'd ever actually expected to hold her again. I had assumed that all of our memories, everything that had occurred, had been purely a figment of my imagination. But now that I was looking at her in my arms? Well, there was nothing imaginary about the woman who I had loved from a young boy. Neither of us were children anymore though, and as I carried her over the walkway towards her bed, I felt a painful surge of heartbreak that I no longer knew her.

That wasn't completely true.

Despite our families not allowing the three of us heirs to hang out, which cut off my access to Bexley, I had found a way to keep in contact with her. Something that wouldn't stay a secret for very long, if I had to guess —the nickname alone had been a dead giveaway. Something I wouldn't have minded—I had no problem explaining I'd traveled territories once a week to leave small notes to her—but what I did mind was possibly causing her pain when she began to question why I would do something like that.

This game we were playing required a delicate balance, and that wasn't my specialty. Rather the opposite.

A low rumble broke from my throat as I walked into her room and found Jagger and Gage both standing there, waiting for me. I ignored them, gently laying her down and wrapping a blanket around her form before pressing a kiss to the top of her head. The action should have been surprising, but instead it felt totally natural.

When she mumbled my name, I fought the urge to join her, knowing I needed to talk to the others first. I broke away from her, following the others into the main room, gently closing the bedroom door behind me.

"Late arrival—what happened?" Gage asked as Jagger poured both of us a drink. I wouldn't lie, it was good to be around the two of them again. The summer had been far longer than I anticipated, and I'd spent half of each week traveling through the Bronzeheart clan territory just to be close to Bexley.

Even if she didn't realize it.

Despite our families not allowing us to communicate or hang out as we had before, we had maintained our friendship, and in the last year, we'd grown closer than ever. Mostly because of the decision we had made about the woman we'd all fought over when she was a young girl growing up with us.

At first, we had thought the solution was letting her pick, but while we didn't know a thing about dating at the time—I was barely ten, Gage and Jagger only nine—she had completely nixed that idea. So we had argued and fought over spending time with her, trying at a young age to assert dominance over one another. I had no doubt we would have figured it out and stopped fighting...but then we lost Bexley. Not actually lost her—well, for more than a night—but lost the part of her that remembered that.

That remembered us.

Now we were more unified than ever, not only to protect her, but because we knew the truth. Not only of who she was in this world, but what she was to us, even if she didn't realize it yet. Even if she *couldn't* realize it because of the spell that bound her memories. The spell kept her and us from everything. Her magic and body remembered us, the comfort and instant trust showcasing that, but her head and emotions had been twisted to not even recognize Jagger and me—something that hurt far more than I could ever describe.

"Held up. My father had a late meeting." I shook my head. "Believe me, I wanted to be here." I would have loved to see her right away, watching her reaction to campus, but walking out of the shower to find her curled up in my armchair was like a fucking dream.

I'd thought I was imagining her at first.

"We have to figure this out, and soon." Jagger looked stressed, sitting on the couch. "I don't disagree with your move to mark her officially—"

"You marked her?" I demanded of Gage.

"Calm down, it's not a mating mark," he rumbled. "Just a bracelet."

Thank fuck, because I would have killed him. I understood it wasn't a reasonable thought process, but the bastard had spent years with her, so if anyone was marking Bexley... Well, I wanted it to be me. I wanted to be selfish and have her give me that, at least for the first time.

"But because of that," Jagger continued, "someone will say something. I saw how easily she was triggered today. Mentioning anything about her past causes her to knock out because of the pain—"

He cut off, sounding panicked. I looked at Gage, his face filled with agony.

"Is that really how bad it is?" I questioned.

"Worse."

"So what do we do?" I tried to remain analytical, wanting to solve the problem before I gave in to the strong emotions slamming into me.

"We find a way to make her shift," Jagger said. "Somehow."

"And we keep as quiet as fucking possible about anything that could cause her to black out," Gage growled, looking at Jagger, who grunted. I was positive Jagger hadn't done it on purpose, but I still didn't like the idea that it had happened to any extent.

"Which reminds me, you broke the rules." Jagger narrowed his eyes at me. "Fucking letters?"

"Notes," I corrected, finding it both annoying and funny they knew. "They were notes." Notes that had tethered me to my sanity for the past few years.

"I figured those were from you," Gage said, sipping on his drink. "You're not any better, Jagger—you think she didn't ask about the constant delivery of flowers? I had to tell her that was the norm."

"That's plausible," he grunted.

Gage chuckled. "Yeah, hate to tell you, but an entire room filled with fresh flowers daily, even for the Bronze-hearts, is not the norm. But she did like them, so that's good."

I ran a hand over my face in thought, ignoring their back and forth. "Because of the mark you put on her, people are going to assume she's a female dragon. We have to be careful because of the wolves."

"Her safety here is of the utmost importance," Gage agreed. "There was no way to hide them thinking she's a female dragon, and despite the dangers associated with that, the bigger issue is keeping them from knowing the full truth of the situation—else I'm not positive we'll be able to stay here. We don't have confirmation on who it was that night—it could have been any of their pack leaders."

Standing up, I let out a frustrated breath and neared the balcony doors, stepping out. I closed my eyes, remembering times far simpler than this when it was easy to express to her exactly how I felt without potentially causing her harm...

Although, it hadn't been like that at first.

"Stand up straighter." My father's voice had me nearly rolling my eyes, but when a hard hit came to my back, I straightened, trying to not wince. One day. *One day I would be stronger than him so he couldn't push me around. It never got bad, but I had a feeling that it did*

with my mom. Not that she would ever admit to it, but I heard her tears sometimes at night.

One day I was going to be able to step in and help her.

"Jagger and Gage are here," my mom said with a calm tone. "Go on and talk to them, honey. It's important to make friends."

She didn't have to tell me twice. I had known my friends for what felt like forever, despite only being eight. When I reached them though, I noticed they were both huddled around a smaller figure. Now, I was fairly large for my age, and while both Jagger and Gage were a year younger than myself, we all tended to be around the same size.

Which is why the contrast of the small figure they were talking to was so shocking.

"Jagger, Gage," I said, trying to draw their attention. They turned to look at me and revealed the smallest little fairy-like girl I'd ever come across. My family didn't come to events often, but I had never seen this girl, and I would have remembered her—she looked like an angel.

Her golden hair was almost down to her waist, and she was wearing a gold sparkly dress that floated around her. She seemed about two years younger than me, and when she looked directly at me, gold eyes meeting my *own, it was like a straight shot to my chest, making it squeeze uncomfortably.*

"Hi." Her voice was soft and upbeat.

"Hi," I answered as she stepped forward and put out her hand.

"I'm Bexley, but you can call me Bex," she announced as I met her hand.

Bex. *Somehow I knew I would never forget that name.*

From that point on, for nearly four years, our friendship was almost unbreakable. Well, not completely unbreakable, because we used to fight over her attention, but looking back on it, that had been nothing. In fact, I was now understanding that she'd been right all along for getting mad at us when we demanded she had to choose. Why should Bex have to choose? Why couldn't she have everything in this goddamn world?

Turning back inside, both Jagger and Gage were talking in low tones, probably considering different ways to inspire her shift. I didn't have the emotional capacity to do that right now though. There was only one thing I wanted, and instead of denying myself it, I walked right into her room and moved towards the bed. Instantly, I noticed that she had moved, kicking away the blankets and stretching out like a kitten.

I eyed the spot next to her, glad Gage had this place redone to fit her massive bed, before saying 'fuck it' and joining her. The mattress dipped under my weight, and I laid out next to her, my gaze on the ceiling until my eyes grew heavy, just enjoying the scent of her jasmine perfume.

Which was why I so easily fell asleep despite being something of an insomniac.

My sleep was dreamless and heavy, the only thing waking me up eventually a subtle tap on my face. I blinked my eyes open and found a gorgeous golden-haired angel looking down at me from where she sat on the bed.

Confusion hit me as I realized that it was morning. I'd never woken up and left—no, I was still right where I'd fallen asleep next to her. I wasn't exactly positive how I was going to explain this one.

"Good morning," she sang sweetly, intertwining her fingers nervously, the golden sunlight surrounding her in a glow. "I didn't want to wake you up, but I also didn't want you to be late if you had class. Honestly, I'm just so glad I didn't imagine last night—that would have been incredibly awkward."

I offered her a smile, a rumble that was nearly a laugh coming up my throat. Why was she so adorable? I mean, it was one thing that the woman was beautiful and, according to her test scores, brilliant, but also adorable? Quirky? Made me smile with just a few words? Yeah, I was fucked.

"You didn't imagine me." I sat up, the blanket falling off my chest, and her eyes following its progress. My chest, which was covered in scars from training, made me momentarily insecure. Well, until her pupils dilated and her breath caught, her cheeks flushing bright pink. Sweet fates, I wasn't going to last minutes around this woman without attacking her. I was suddenly wondering where Gage had found his level of patience that he'd maintained for nearly eight years.

A rumble broke from my throat as the sweet scent of her desire filled the air around me, and my cock, which was already partly hard from sleeping in the same bed as her, grew uncomfortably rigid. Her eyes flashed back up to mine as she drew her bottom lip in. Fuck. This woman had no idea how she looked, how fucking appealing she was.

"I—" She paused, her breath catching as she examined my expression with both heat and a bit of caution.

It was like she could feel my dragon surging inside of me, threatening to break out. A part of her, even small, knew that would mean something for her. The control I was attempting to maintain wasn't sustainable, I knew that, but I tried to stay as still as possible. Then her large gold eyes trailed down to where I was obviously extremely hard.

When her nipples tightened against her silk top in reaction, I lost it.

Gage may have had control enough to not touch her like she was ours, but I did not. I pinned her to the bed in an instant, keeping her hot body underneath mine as she whimpered, feeling how hard I was against her squirming frame. I kept myself there, my hands wrapped around her wrists that I'd positioned over her head, looking over every inch of her.

I wanted to peel that silk off of her with my damn teeth.

"Breaker," she whimpered, my name causing me to let out an actual growl.

I gently clasped her jaw in one hand and looked down at her perfect lips before deciding that I was going to take what was mine.

Chapter 11

Bexley

I'd tried to never imagine my first kiss before.

Of course, I'd imagined a lot of other stuff, mostly with Gage...but my first kiss had felt important. Almost sacred. I knew it would be the first time I felt a strong connection with someone, and I was one hundred percent right.

Breaker's lips were softer than I expected, and when he swept down and claimed my mouth in a kiss, a sound, nearly a moan, came from my throat as a wave of physical and emotional pleasure swept through me. I didn't hesitate to kiss him back, despite being unpracticed. My fingers went into his hair, and I mimicked his movements as he devoured my mouth, causing my entire body to well with heat.

I had been turned on when I found him in my bed,

immediately taken away by how beautiful he was, a vicious warrior with scars along his golden torso. But then I'd watched his reaction to me and how hard he'd gotten, making my desire amp up tenfold. I felt my legs wrap around his hips as he ground into me, the movement causing friction against my center and a swell of pleasure to build up.

I didn't know what I needed, but I had a feeling that he could give it to me.

I had a feeling Breaker could give me a lot of pleasure, and I wanted it all.

When he ripped his lips away from mine, I was out of breath and staring up at him with wide eyes, feeling flushed as a smile crawled onto my mouth. I momentarily worried he would apologize like Gage, but instead he just leaned back down and placed a soft kiss on my lips.

"What was that?" I asked breathlessly.

"Proving that you belong to me, *mo chuisle*," he replied softly. My toes curled as he brushed his nose against mine before letting out a grunt and sitting back. "And because of that, I can't let you be late for your first day."

Despite the pout slipping onto my lips, I couldn't help but find it amazing that he cared about that. I wasn't positive what I'd expected Breaker to be like, especially after our odd first encounter last night...but it wasn't this. I could feel his magic wrapping around me with warmth and a coating of protectiveness that I loved.

"It feels so early..." I complained. I was already wide awake, but I'd find any excuse to stay in bed with him. My words had him chuckling, and it was such an amazing sound that I didn't even mind as he pulled me from bed. I let out a surprised squeak as he carried me in a bridal hold, before setting me down at the bathroom and nodding towards it.

"Go get ready," he instructed. "I will make coffee after I get changed." His mismatched eyes were filled with so much happiness that it almost made me breathless. Yeah, I had no idea what to make of this man... Well, except that I loved this. Whatever *this* was.

I mumbled another half-hearted complaint about leaving bed as he slipped out of my dorm, jogging across the bridge towards his own, but I ultimately listened, deciding to take a quick shower. I should have taken a bath last night, but now it was officially on the agenda for tonight, following my classes. After a nice hot shower, having scrubbed my hair, I stepped out and wrapped myself up in a towel, walking up to the mirror and examining my face. I normally slept fine, but I had to admit I looked extremely well-rested today.

Not knowing how much time I had, I got ready, blow-drying my hair straight and applying some light makeup before slipping on a robe. I peeked out, disappointed to not see Breaker, but deciding it was a good opportunity to get dressed. Not that I would have minded being caught in a robe...

My fingers skimmed over my lips as I flushed, unable to believe I'd *finally* had my first kiss.

I noticed that my bedroom still smelled faintly of his vanilla scent, and instead of opening the balcony doors, I kept them closed, wanting it to last. I straightened my bed up and then went to my closet, looking over my selection as I tried to figure out what the 'right' option was for the first day of class. On one hand, everyone seemed rather casual... On the other hand, I literally didn't have any casual clothes. Shrugging to myself, I grabbed my favorite outfit and laid it out on the bed, looking out at the skies, which were surprisingly sunny considering last night. I had thought for sure we would get more of a storm... But then again, I was always hoping for a storm.

I would love to spend the afternoon curled up with...the three of them? Was that how I felt? Well, if it wasn't, it sure as heck had been how I'd been acting. My cheeks flushed, trying to not overthink my actions. For whatever reason, these other two men, nearly strangers, were inspiring a reaction in me, and since Gage was friends with them... I could trust them, right?

I had to hope that was the case.

Slipping on pale yellow panties and a bra, I wiggled into a pair of pink and gray plaid cropped pants, paired with a cashmere light pink sweater that hung loosely around me, a bit oversized. I slipped on a pair of pearly high heel ankle boots that had faux fur on the inside and then slipped on a pair of diamond earrings Mrs. Bronzeheart had gotten me last holiday season. I looked at myself in the large mirror inside the closet and smiled happily, grabbing my bag and sorting through some of the school supplies I'd brought with me. Once I was all settled and good to go, I walked back out into the room, expecting to see Breaker.

Instead, I found a note.

Have to handle something, mo chuisle.
    Wait for one of the others to walk you to class.
    See you soon.

When had he stopped here? Why hadn't he said anything? I was a bit disappointed he didn't plan on walking me to class, but more than anything, I felt shocked. I mean... Was I crazy, or was this messy scrawl familiar? I looked back at my room and considered comparing the handwriting to the box of notes in my closet.

Maybe I was creating connections where they didn't exist. I mean, why would Breaker be my pen pal? That made no sense at all... Right? Deciding to handle it later, I tucked it into my pocket and looked around for my packet, knowing I needed to at least check the time of my first class while waiting for Gage, or possibly Jagger.

I smiled, finding the paper in question on the coffee table. My classes for the day were circled with a red pen, no doubt courtesy of Jagger. *DIA Introduction & Basics* and *Understanding & Communicating with Your Animal Counterpart.*

That seemed like a good schedule for the first day, right? I was really looking for someone to assure me of that.

After looking through my schedule for the rest of the week and waiting about ten minutes, I glanced at the clock and then at the door, knowing that if I didn't leave now I probably wouldn't have breakfast. Something that was absolutely not an option if I wanted my stomach to stay quiet during my morning lessons. My eyes widened at that thought—fates, *talk about embarrassing.*

Nibbling my lip, I decided I was hungry enough to

just go get food myself. I let out a frustrated huff at having to leave without them, writing out a quick note and placing it on the counter before moving to the elevator.

As it took me down several stories, I found myself imagining what it would be like to fly down each morning instead. I bet it was amazing. Not for the first time, I closed my eyes and tried to search for that part of myself, the one lodged deep inside that was supposed to be attached to my animal. Everyone told me I was a shifter, but I'd never had proof of that. I mean, literally, I didn't have an animal... I let out a sigh, not feeling anything there but shallow disappointment.

When I stepped out into the early morning air, I put my head back and let the sunshine warm my skin. I could feel my thoughts getting dark with disappointment, but I wasn't going to let my insecurities mar my first day of class. No, that was not how I was going to start all of this out. The warmth in my chest grew with conviction as I felt a surge of happiness and excitement for the day blast through me.

A rustling noise drew my attention. I looked around the forested path I was on, feeling eyes on me. I considered calling out, but chalking it up to nerves, I continued down the path a bit. When I heard someone following me, I took a few more steps before turning sharply, my eyebrows shooting up.

Honestly, I wasn't positive about what or who I'd expected to see...but a large wolf with auburn fur was *totally* not it. I tilted my head, offering a small smile, noticing that despite being intimidating size-wise, he seemed friendly? Almost? I knew that it wasn't a good idea to interact with shifters I didn't know, but I couldn't help myself.

"Good morning," I offered in an affable manner.

The wolf tilted its head curiously before offering me a small head nod and then disappearing again, leaving me smiling a bit. I had never had a lot of friends before—like I mentioned, there weren't many I could trust—and while Gage was my best friend, I could tell that the feelings I had for him and the other two would never be *just* friendly. Maybe making friends here wouldn't be difficult at all; maybe it would keep my mind off of what I could never have.

Turning on my heels and pushing the incident from my mind, I followed the pathway to arrive at the large building that contained the dining hall. I happily made my way up the back steps and through the large arches, the crowded student area outside of the dining hall buzzing with excitement. There were so many students, and all at once I was hit by so many scents that I felt like I was almost high on magic. When was the last time I'd even been around this many people? It was both overwhelming and wonderful at the same time.

Moving through the crowd, I walked into the dining hall by myself and felt that surge of nervousness I couldn't seem to banish. I had no one to sit with, unfortunately, but I tried not to dwell on that, hoping no one would notice me. Those hopes were dashed, though, when everyone started to stare at me. I kept my gaze forward, feeling my cheeks heat, continuously telling myself that once I got food, I could get out of here.

When a chest appeared in front of me, I almost jolted back, but a large hand clasped my waist, causing me to look up. Jagger.

A goofy smile pressed to my lips before my brow furrowed. Why did he look so unhappy?

"What are you doing, Bex?"

I could hear people talking in whispers around us, most likely about us, and I felt a weird pang of self-consciousness. "Eating breakfast... Well, trying to."

"I could have brought you something," he gritted out, glancing over my head. "You shouldn't be in here."

Well, then. I blinked at his words and drew my bottom lip in, not knowing how to respond to what felt like cruel words. I had no idea how he meant them, but when my eyes started to sting, he immediately grasped my chin, his eyebrows pinching in confusion.

"Why are you crying?"

"You don't want me here," I murmured.

His eyebrows shot up. "Little treasure, I promise you it is not that. You just have no idea how much attention you attract."

"But why is that my fault?" I countered. "I still need to eat."

Darkness flashed in his gaze. "I never said it was your fault."

"So I can get breakfast then? Also coffee. I didn't grab any before leaving the dorm." I offered him a small smile, trying to banish the tension between us while ignoring the reminder that Breaker had promised to get me coffee and then all but disappeared. "Want to come with me?"

"I shouldn't," he said, apology clear in his tone. "It will only bring more attention to you."

"Okay." I nodded and tried to slip past him, not wanting him to see my disappointment, but his hand almost immediately wrapped around my center, his nose burying in my hair.

"You are making all of this very complicated."

I turned into him, tilting my head back. "Are you embarrassed by me?"

There! That was easy, right?

"What?" He went wide-eyed.

"Why else would you be worried about me being here? I mean, if you say it's not about wanting me to be here, are you sure it's not about being embarrassed to be seen around me? I understand the living arrangements aren't the best, but that's not your fault—"

Jagger let out a growl and cupped my face gently. "Let's get one thing straight."

"Listening," I murmured, his eyes flashing silver with intensity.

"I want you here. Always. I am *never* embarrassed by you. I am being a possessive bastard and don't want these other fuckers looking at you—that is the problem here, not you."

Oh. I offered a small surprised smile. "You're possessive over me?"

Jagger let out a low rumble. "Yes, and I know the vipers that are in this damn place—"

"Jagger." The feminine voice had my metaphorical hairs standing on end as I leaned into my dragon, a woman approaching us from a crowded table that was watching us with interest. Wait...had I said *my* dragon? Crap. Although...he *was* still holding me, and considering how tight his grip was, I didn't think he planned on letting go any time soon.

"Diane." Jagger's tone was indifferent; if anything, it was heavy with boredom.

The gorgeous brunette looked between the two of us, appearing somehow effortlessly beautiful and casual at the same time. I noticed that despite wearing sneakers, she was staring down at me, and her eyes were critical as she analyzed each factor of my existence. At least that's what it felt like. Instead of shrinking though, I narrowed my eyes at her, keeping eye contact despite a growl breaking from her chest.

In theory, she should have been threatening, yet instead I only felt annoyed she was disrupting my time with Jagger.

"She's not important to you," Jagger bit out, and I realized something was wrong. His polished tone was gone, and his snapped reply had her stepping back, her face paling. Unfortunately, the smile that followed once she'd pulled herself together had me knowing that Jagger's intense reaction had been exactly what she was looking for.

"Oh, I think she is," the woman purred, still looking a bit cautious before meeting my gaze. "Until later then."

When she walked past us, I realized I'd been holding my breath, and I muttered a frustrated curse under my breath, hoping I didn't look completely weak.

"Vipers. Those are vipers," Jagger said when I looked back to him. "Negative attention is why I am worried about you being here, little treasure. I want this experience to be good for you."

I nodded in understanding, unable to deny the fact that at his core, the man was sweet. "Well... Sounds like we got the bad part out of the way. Should we get coffee first?"

He offered me a slow smile, a dimple forming on his right cheek that I found myself focusing on. When he spoke, he still sounded stressed, but a bit less than before. "Sure. Let's see how you drink your coffee. I want to know if my guess is right."

"Well, what's your guess?" I asked as we reached the coffee bar.

"Sugar and lots of peppermint creamer," he mused as my eyes went wide. I would have asked how he knew that, but soon my name was echoing through the room.

"Bex!" *Gage.*

I turned to see the man striding towards me through the dining hall, looking panicked and not seeming to care about everyone staring. In fact, when I did meet a few gazes, I found myself surprised by the level of shock there, but more so, the anger. There seemed to be a lot of narrowed looks being sent my way as whispers filled the room.

What had I done? Or was it Gage they were mad at? I knew something was up, but I didn't have time to question it as my best friend closed the distance between us.

Jagger continued to make my coffee as I offered Gage a sweet smile, unable to say anything before I was promptly swept off the floor. I let out a surprised gasp as I naturally wrapped my legs around his massive frame and he buried his nose against my throat. I had expected a lot, but not this level of PDA—I loved it, my arms tightening around him almost possessively as I noticed the amount of females staring at both him and Jagger.

Actually, there was nothing 'almost' about it. I was totally being possessive. Why the heck did they have to look at them anyway? I found myself wishing they would mind their own business, despite it being a rather rude thought.

"I could kill Breaker for leaving you alone," he growled. "I was so worried, cupcake."

"I was hungry," I pointed out, "and I didn't want to be late for class. He told me to wait, but I left a note."

"We need more than snacks for the room, that way she can eat breakfast there," Jagger commented. Gage let me down, and I took the cup of coffee Jagger offered, letting out a happy hum as I took a sip.

"This is amazing," I told him as he smiled again—I was really hoping it was going to become a pattern. I took a risk and went up on my toes and kissed his cheek, surprise at my action coating his features.

"You always sleep in, Bex." Gage scowled, still clearly caught up on this.

"I'm a new woman," I pointed out in a teasing way, diverting my eyes before I added the next part. "Plus, Breaker slept in my bed last night, so I woke up and wanted to talk to him."

Gage let out a low rumble. "And what did Breaker say?"

"Not much." I shrugged before offering, "He did kiss me though."

Now, why had I said that? I stared down at my coffee as I felt both of them go perfectly still. I mean, I knew why I had said it, but now I was wondering if it had been a good idea.

I just found myself a bit frustrated since yesterday with Gage... And then Jagger saying he was possessive... It was a confusing situation that I had no experience handling, and I constantly felt like I didn't have all the information I needed.

Jagger wrapped a hand around my waist as Gage tilted my chin up with a finger, his eyes flashing pure bronze. I didn't think he was mad, but he seemed to be actively trying to control his emotions. "He took your first kiss?"

"Well, it's not really taking it if I gave it to him..."

Gage continued to stare at me, his entire body tensing before looking at Jagger, seeming to communicate something in yet another one of those irritating silent conversations. "I'm going to get you food, cupcake. Sit with Jagger."

He was gone then, and I arched a brow, looking up at Jagger. "Is he mad?"

Jagger had a ghost of a smile on his lips. "I think you know he's not mad, exactly."

"I don't know what he is because he won't tell me," I grumbled.

Jagger chuckled softly this time, leading me to a table. "I have no doubt you will find out soon, little treasure."

I hoped he was right, because I was finding that my patience when it came to all these new discoveries was limited.

Chapter 12

Bexley

I was regretting the large breakfast I'd just had.

Not because it hadn't been wonderful, but because it had left me sleepy. Shortly after sitting down, Jagger had left, murmuring something about class and leaving me with Gage. I wouldn't say things were off between us, because that wasn't exactly true...but there was a strained undertone to our relationship that hadn't been there before, and I wasn't positive what to do about it.

Yet instead of bringing anything up, in large part because I was a chicken, I ate my food as he watched, not even touching his coffee. After finishing half my plate, I finally looked up and offered him a curious look, wondering what he was so deep in thought about.

"What?" I asked sincerely.

"Just getting used to you being here," he admitted before adding, as if knowing my insecurities, "I didn't think it would ever happen. I had no doubt you would get in, but it never felt like a reality until now."

"On the first day of classes," I hummed in agreement. I know it probably sounded lame, but since I'd never been to a real school before with classmates, I was really excited. I had a feeling Gage could tell that, because he didn't even tell me I was drinking too much coffee when I stole his mug.

After finishing my plate, I hopped up and then looked down at him, his gaze running over my outfit in what looked like appreciation before he grunted and stood himself, towering over me. I looked down at his hand momentarily. I knew we'd held hands before on the estate, but that was different. This time I could feel eyes on us, and I didn't want Gage to have to explain...

He grabbed my hand and took my bag, slinging it over his other shoulder. I couldn't help the smile that filled my face as I snuggled up close to him as he walked us out of the dining hall, my chest warm and happy. I let out a soft hum under my breath as we left the building and crossed into the courtyard.

"Maybe you shouldn't have had that second cup of coffee." Gage chuckled softly.

I turned into him, coming to a stop about halfway towards the rather unique classrooms on the other end. My head fell back as I offered him a curious smile. "What? Why?" I tried to not steal his coffee all the time, but I wouldn't lie, it was a bit difficult when I was craving an extra cup, especially since we drank ours exactly the same...

I tilted my head, realizing that I had never seen him finish a cup of coffee. My mouth opened in shock, and it was his turn to look surprised.

"What?"

"Do you even drink coffee?"

His smile was gorgeous as he flashed a set of perfectly white teeth. "Not really, especially since you have been stealing it every morning for years."

I had. That was an accurate statement.

I couldn't help the smile forming on my face. "And you let me have it?"

His large hand came up to cup my jaw. "I'll give you anything you want, Bex."

The moment was filled with intensity between us, and I finally blinked, pulling out of it as someone shouted to another student nearby. The frustrated sound emanating from Gage's chest had me thinking he had felt the moment as well. Something was changing between the two of us, and I was both cautious and wanting to run head-first into it, eager to discover this other side of Gage.

When he began leading me towards the large triangle-shaped buildings bordering the entrance of the sector, I tried to decide whether or not to bring up his reaction to the kiss.

"What are you thinking about?" he demanded. The man was constantly in tune with my thoughts and emotions—sometimes I wondered if he was a mind reader.

"Honestly?"

"Always."

"Trying to figure out your reaction to Breaker kissing me."

Gage's eyes flashed pure bronze and stayed that way as he evaluated my expression before letting out a low, throaty rumble.

"See?" I pointed out. "You're getting all upset—"

"Protective. I'm protective over you," he bit out, running a hand through his hair, his normal level of control seeming to hang right on the edge.

"Oh." I blinked, feeling a surge of disappointment. Why had I thought it was more than that? Gage made a concerned noise as he reached out for my hand, but I shifted slightly away from him.

"Cupcake." The warning had me wanting to escape

so he couldn't question me. I knew he would, and I knew I wouldn't be able to lie. The only reason Gage hadn't found out about my feelings for him was because he hadn't asked. If he asked, I was totally screwed.

"No, it makes complete sense!" I squeaked, my cheeks turning red in embarrassment. "I actually need to get to class—*Gage!*"

The man lifted me up so that I was suspended in the air in front of him, staring into his gorgeous green eyes. I didn't bother trying to get out of his grip as he exhaled, seeming to try to get a hold on his emotions. I both wanted to soothe the tension out of him and run into class to avoid the embarrassment of hearing what he had to say.

"It is so much more than that," he admitted softly. "So much more, Bex. But for now, I need you to not question it. Not until I figure out how to make this right."

"Make it right?"

"Make it right."

After examining his expression, seeing only the truth there, I nodded slowly and he set me down, putting my backpack on my shoulder. His voice rough as he once again took my hand and led me towards the building. "Come on, cupcake."

I had no idea what to make of my best friend

anymore. Seriously, I'd never seen him acting this way, and it both excited me and made me nervous. I wanted to question him, but I also trusted him, so if he said we needed to wait for him to 'make it right,' then I would wait...for now, at least. Besides, my attention was snagged as I looked ahead to where the door stood open, the glass walls allowing me to see students gathering and grouping up in the classroom.

Immediately, I noticed the thing that stood out.

A small woman with bright pink hair and a stature even smaller than mine was in the corner of the classroom, closest to the exit, clearly avoiding everyone else. I felt a sense of defensiveness as I wondered if she was scared. I didn't like that at all.

Frustration welled through me as I realized that the other shifters seemed to be purposefully excluding her. Was this how people normally behaved? I had never been around a lot of people in general, but if it was... Well, this sucked.

Gage wrapped a hand around my hip and spoke quietly. "Predatory shifters don't normally get along with other types of shifters. It appears that your class has a large amount of the first."

Why did I feel like that spelled trouble for me?

"Well, I'm barely a shifter, so I plan on not acting like a jerk."

A dark noise came from Gage. I looked up at him, my brows scrunched in confusion. "What?"

"You just said you're barely a shifter, cupcake."

"It's true," I said, keeping my chin held up a little bit, "but I'm not going to be ashamed of that." I would secretly feel insecure about it, but I had never been put down or bullied in my life before, and I wasn't going to allow someone to do it to me, or others, now.

Gage's eyes melted into bronze and green swirls as a hint of pride coasted across his face. "Get into class, cupcake. I will be here to pick you up."

"Don't you have class?" I teased.

"Not one that is more important than you." Gage's tone was slightly growly as he nodded towards the door, my face hot from blushing like a total weirdo.

"See you soon," I murmured and walked up the steps, feeling exhilarated about this change between Gage and me. Although, that feeling was quickly over-shadowed when I could feel so many different eyes on me at once.

I had no doubt that, much like the pink-haired woman, I would be shunned, so I didn't even bother trying with the large group. Not that I would want to be friends with people like that in the first place. I walked towards her, and her massive blue eyes shot up to regard me with unease, her nervous energy filling the space.

"Hey." I offered a small smile. "Mind if I sit?"

"S-sure." She nodded, looking on edge. Her eyes kept darting to the larger group as if she was expecting them to do something. I slid into the chair, hooking my backpack over the seat and offering her an understanding look.

"They seem like jerks, if it's any consolation."

Her eyes went wide. "Aren't you one of them?"

"One of what?"

"A predatory shifter?" she asked, confused, as my temple pulsed slightly. I brought a hand up to it but managed to ignore it and answer her question.

"Nope, have never shifted," I admitted honestly.

Her eyebrows shot up. "Oh. I'm sorry, that was rude of me. I just assumed because you live with the dragons."

"Yeah..." I hedged, "That's sort of a weird situation."

The girl examined my expression before nodding. "I understand."

And even if she didn't, I appreciated that she didn't push the conversation.

"My name is Bexley." I offered my hand as she met it. "But call me Bex."

"Oh, I know! Everyone knows your name," she explained, promptly turning bright pink. "Fates, I am so awkward. Sorry."

"Not at all," I assured her and then admitted, "Gage and the two others don't exactly do anything around here that goes unnoticed."

"You're not wrong," she agreed before finally saying, "And my name is Rachel, by the way!"

Before we could exchange more pleasantries, the door closed, and both of our heads turned to see a large male, obviously the professor by how he was dressed, walking towards the front of the room. We turned in our seats towards the front as Rachel made a concerned noise. I arched a brow, realizing there was slight fear associated with her reaction, but something else as well.

I had to admit, the man was intimidating...but so were the dragons I lived with, so maybe I was biased? When he turned towards the front, putting down his bag on the desk and shrugging off his jacket, I realized he was sort of handsome. I heard Rachel mutter a curse and sink further down into her chair as the professor's head snapped up.

My eyes widened at the instant reaction. The man froze up, staring at Rachel for what felt like five minutes. The rest of the class began to grow a bit anxious and looked back here to see what was going on. Something that caused him to pull his gaze away, his booming voice drawing attention and allowing me to check on my friend. My friend, whose face was bright pink and whose magic was bouncing around the space almost manically. What in the heck was going on?

"You good?" I whispered, ignoring his words to the rest of the class.

"Sort of. I'll explain later," she murmured. I nodded and then looked forward. Something was for sure up, but it didn't seem like a major problem right now if she was willing to ignore it.

"I am Professor Clanguard," the man up front explained. "I will be your professor for your introductory first-year class: *Dark Imaginarium Academy History & Basics*. We will spend the semester going over the rules for the academy and the history of how we came to be the institute you are familiar with today. Additionally, I hope to fit in a discussion about the planes of existence. I know a lot of shifter schools don't emphasize or seem to care that we have several planes of existence above and below us..." he drew out, looking frustrated, "but I do."

I didn't know what other schools were like and how much they taught, but luckily, during our extensive tutoring sessions, I had been briefed on all of that information. Not that I minded a refresher.

Then again, I had also traveled to far more places with the Bronzehearts than a lot of the students here. I knew that was a privilege associated with the position of

Gage's clan, and it had given me a far easier geographic reference than a map.

A map that was currently being passed out.

I tilted my head, examining the detailed illustration, mainly focusing my attention on Praeditus. Dark Imaginarium Academy was located near the center of the plane, although the specific position of it was highly safeguarded. The rest of the plane was focused around several different territories, one for each of the magical beings that we knew to exist: demigods, shifters, vampires, demons, fae, and witches.

All of which I found extremely fascinating and hoped to meet while here. Although, the academy had seemed to follow suit in separating all of us, which was a bit disappointing. I'd always thought vampires were really cool, at least from what I'd learned about them, so I was still hoping I'd get to meet some.

My gaze traveled up to the plane of existence where the gods and goddesses ruled: Divinus. I'd never been up there, and from the conversations I'd heard between Mr. and Mrs. Bronzeheart, I wasn't positive I wanted to. Besides, while we had access to a lot, traveling different planes was still difficult because you had to use veils, which could only be opened through portals like the one the headmistress used.

So that probably wouldn't happen any time soon.

Which was a tiny bit of a shame, because below us was Ordinarius, where the humans resided. *Talk about a fascinating group.* I mean, seriously, how an entire population of individuals lived—and thrived—without magic was a mystery to me! Shifters usually didn't even have that much magic outside of their connection with their animal, but none at all? I suppose... Well, I suppose I was the closest thing to being 'human,' wasn't I?

That realization was a mixture of somewhat entertaining and depressing—not a fun mixture at all. Shaking the frustration that welled through me, I looked at the final plane: Hell. I knew the humans didn't like it very much, but the rulers there had been fundamental to establishing the academy. At least that was what I'd been told.

Maybe I'd talk to the Bronzehearts about taking a trip down there. Gage and I could even say it was for school, and it wouldn't be a complete lie! It would also be a super cool vacation... Instantly, I thought about inviting Breaker and Jagger. That seemed to be the natural extension of my idea, the logical next step, as if I wasn't meant to question it. As if they were just meant to be there with me. I nearly shook my head at that. Why was I being so clingy?

I mean what else did I call it besides that?

"Want to be partners?" Rachel asked softly, pulling my attention.

"Sure!" I nodded and then felt an embarrassed smile slip onto my face. "For what?"

She laughed. "We have to create a 3D model based on the universe image by next week. It seems fun."

That actually did seem fun.

When a shadow came over the desk, I stilled before looking up to find a guy there. I frowned in confusion, because I realized at that moment how little I interacted with males outside of Gage, and now my other roommates. I didn't really know what to say to him, and the look he was giving me wasn't exactly friendly. At least, not *just* friendly. I didn't say anything, offering the guy a blank look as he plastered a charming smile on his face, which failed to disguise the darkness in his gaze.

"You're Bexley, right?"

"Sure am," I responded.

"Right." He nodded. "My name is Ioan."

"Nice to meet you," I offered. Rachel seemed to sink in her seat to get away from him, but he barely noticed.

"I was wondering if you wanted to be partners." The man seemed supremely confident that I would want to be, his cocky smile feeling off. It was sexy when Gage looked like that, but this guy seemed to just be...I don't know, there was just something off about him. His blonde hair was messy, and his eyes were completely black and focused on me, almost to the point that it was unnerving.

"No thank you, I'm working with Rachel."

Surprise covered his face. "No...*thank you?*"

I felt like I'd been pretty clear, but instead he was staring at me in shock.

"Back to your seat," our professor demanded. "No means no, Ioan."

The guy's face turned red as he stomped away, leaving me to look at Rachel, who was looking at me in disbelief. "What?"

"Just can't believe you said no to him," she murmured.

"I'm already partners with you," I stated simply. Rachel's smile was filled with warmth as if I had said something important to her. "Now, let's talk about this model."

Chapter 13

Bexley

Class went by far faster than I'd expected, and by the end of it, Rachel and I had established exactly how we were going to put the model together. We planned to meet sometime this weekend to actually construct it, but other than that, the project seemed fairly simple.

"Did you hear about the party tonight?" Her question had me looking up as both of us put away our books and papers, waiting to be dismissed from class. I could tell she was eager to get out of here, and I knew she probably didn't want to talk to our professor. I didn't know what was going on between them, but I did know that he was still staring at her.

"Party?" I asked curiously.

I'd never been to a party before, outside of formal

events, let alone one at an academy... Would Gage want to come with? Jagger? Breaker? Or would they find that lame? They had obviously been here longer than myself, so if parties were a normal occurrence, they probably wouldn't want to go.

"Yep." She nodded and then spoke more quietly. "The demon sector is where it's held, you just have to sneak through the pavilion and go over there. I was hoping to go; a few of the girls from my dorm are. You want to join?"

I grinned, excited about the concept. "Absolutely, I may have to meet you there, but I am definitely interested."

Rachel seemed thrilled with that, and when our professor announced the end of class, she slipped from the room in the blink of an eye, leaving me staring in confusion. I looked back at our professor, who was stuck talking to a student, even as his eyes tracked her retreating form.

Yep, there was *totally* something going on there.

I needed to tell Gage about that and about meeting a new friend in general. Speaking of which, where was the man? I walked down the steps, ignoring the girls glaring at me and whispering, as I searched the sea of students changing classes for Gage.

Deciding it was better just to stay put, I didn't move

from the stone stairs. What I didn't account for? Ioan seemed to decide that he wasn't finished with our discussion from earlier.

"So, Bexley." Ioan's voice was tense, his tone uncomfortable. "I know you felt like you couldn't ditch the bunny—"

"I didn't feel anything," I noted, holding his gaze. While I could feel dominance seeping off of him, it didn't affect me at all. Maybe it was because I was used to being around such powerful shifters. "I want to work with Rachel."

"Instead of me?" he demanded in a frustrated growl.

"Yes," I communicated clearly. I didn't want to be mean, but I also wasn't going to let him talk about my new friend as if she was disposable as a partner.

He scrutinized me for a moment before seeming to relax slightly, taking a new tactic. "I get it. You have the 'nice girl' vibe about you. How about we grab lunch then? No need to change partners for some stupid class."

"I have another class," I pointed out. "I don't really want—"

Suddenly, Breaker appeared next to me, drawing my attention to his handsome face. Somehow he looked even more gorgeous than when he was in my bed, which was surprising in its own right. His mismatched eyes ran over my expression with affection before he turned his attention to Ioan with a glare. I turned my attention back to the classmate in question and found that he looked paler than before.

"Did you ask her to lunch?" Breaker's voice was a low rumble.

"I did," Ioan said, a slight tremble to his frame.

Breaker's chest produced a dark sound, one that had my skin breaking out into shivers, as he stepped forward and looked down at him. "I highly suggest you fuck off before the others arrive."

Jagger and Gage. I knew without a doubt that was who he was referring to. I smiled to myself, imagining hanging out with all of them at the same time. How did I manage to miss my new roommates in such a short amount of time?

Roommates. I knew that was what they were, but our connection felt like more than that. At least on my end, and maybe that was the problem—everything here was only on my end.

"I don't care—" His voice turned choked as suddenly Gage's large hand gripped the back of his collar and tightened the material around his throat.

Gage looked furious, his gaze completely bronze as it ran over me, as if checking I was okay, before focusing back on Ioan. When a hand slid over my hip, lightly and almost hesitantly, I looked up to find Jagger offering me a ghost of a smile.

Fates. These men were so intense yet so different. It was intoxicating.

Breaker, despite being extremely intimidating, had this softness to him that, while only shown towards me so far, seemed to change him completely. Jagger, while seemingly harsh and cold at first, had a vulnerability to him that I knew was the true him. Gage, whose normal relaxed mannerisms had been exchanged for something else...something more dangerous. Despite it being a bit overwhelming, I was finding that my favorite place to be was surrounded by these men.

Which was a huge problem, considering I shouldn't want them. Not when there was no possibility of a future—I was practically begging for heartbreak on a silver platter. It was clear that Breaker felt something for me. At least a physical reaction, since he'd kissed me, and maybe more because he said that I was his. I also felt like there was something to Jagger saying he was possessive over me, but at the end of the day, none of that mattered.

I wasn't a female dragon. Heck, I was barely a shifter. More so, I wasn't any of their mates. That wasn't a connection easily ignored.

"Leave. Now." Jagger's voice was hard and had me

jolting slightly, his grip tightening as if worried I would try to move.

Ioan narrowed his eyes on me before tugging from Gage's grip and making a break for it. As I watched his retreat, I realized that everyone nearby had watched the spectacle. It was a bit embarrassing. Not their actions—no, those made me feel protected, but I knew this would probably make it look like I was okay with that type of intimidation in general, which wasn't true... Or was it?

Why did it seem so different when they did it compared to others?

I frowned. "I feel like doing that doesn't make us any better than how he and his friends were shunning Rachel."

"What?" Breaker asked.

"The bunny shifter, I assume?" Gage translated. I nodded as he continued, explaining to the others, "She was alone in a group of predatory shifters."

"I don't want to be like that, like them. He was probably trying to make friends." I really didn't think he had been, but I also was wondering if I'd been looking too much into his actions.

"No. He was not." Jagger's voice was edged in frustration, but I didn't think it was at me. "The difference between them shunning a bunny shifter and this is miles wide, little treasure." *There was that nickname.*

"How so?"

The three of them exchanged a look as I waited, but when they didn't say anything, I huffed. "Okay, well, I had handled it just fine in class—"

"In class?" Gage demanded, his jaw clenching.

"Yeah, he wanted to work together."

"One of us should sit in the class with her," Jagger murmured.

"Not a horrible idea," Breaker agreed.

I tugged away from all three of them and held their gazes, trying to figure out if they were serious. In theory I loved the idea of them being in class with me, but I didn't think it was for the right reason. "Listen, I don't know why Ioan was acting like that—"

"Because he wants you."

I froze at Breaker's words and cocked my head. "What?"

"He wants you, Bex," Gage reiterated.

"He didn't want to be friends," Jagger added.

Oh.

I considered what they were saying and nibbled my lip. "Okay, well it doesn't really matter. I didn't want to be friends with him, but that isn't my issue. I don't want you to bully or intimidate anyone, especially not for me. There has to be a better way to handle it." Even though it seemed that was how shifters handled almost everything. "Please? I know you're protective, but I need you to listen to me about this."

There! I was being firm, right?

They exchanged a look again, and then Gage ran a hand over his jaw in thought. "We will do our best, cupcake."

"Unless you are in danger," Breaker qualified.

I nodded and then offered a soft smile, feeling far better. I squeezed Jagger's hand before going up on my toes to press a kiss to Gage's cheek and then slid over to hug Breaker. I was down the steps then, letting out a happy sound before looking back to see all three of them following me.

Were they serious about sitting with me in my next class?

* * *

Unfortunately, they hadn't been, which was a shame since I was almost positive that this was going to be my least favorite class of the semester. I hated that I even had a least favorite to begin with, but it was hard to be excited for a class when I couldn't even participate in it.

Understanding & Communicating With Your Animal Counterpart.

It was essentially focused around meditation as

every other student went through the extensive mental exercises we'd been instructed in to complete the connection to our animal counterparts. I, on the other hand, sat awkwardly in the corner, having given up after about five minutes.

The school and most of the teachers were probably aware that I couldn't shift. Ms. Stagshot had all but said so. Although, to her credit, she hadn't asked me too many questions and had placed me near a large set of windows that faced the forested landscape of campus. I tried looking for my dorm but couldn't see it from here, unfortunately.

Would I ever be able to connect with my animal? Heck, did I even have an animal? A small sigh left my lips as I looked around the classroom of five, the comfortable, cozy space filled with large mats and pillows, similar to a yoga studio.

Closing my eyes, I tried to pull at that part inside of me, the part that was supposed to be tied to my soul, and came back with…nothing. *Absolutely nothing.*

I muttered in exasperation under my breath before rubbing a hand over my face, feeling embarrassed and hoping none of my other classmates realized how inexperienced I was. How much of a failure I was.

I knew that Rachel, who sat a space away from me, was aware of my issue, but she seemed utterly relaxed and zoned into her connection with her bunny. I would admit that I was jealous. Completely and totally jealous.

"Bexley?" Ms. Stagshot appeared in front of me, speaking in a soft whisper and offering me a kind smile.

The woman had a grandmotherly way about her, her gray hair piled on top of her head, and the soft natural fabric shirt and pants she wore made her look like she was in a constant state of relaxation. Her turquoise eyes were soft and understanding as she motioned for me to follow her. I did so, hoping we would step outside to talk. I knew people would find out that I didn't shift, and I knew I said I wouldn't be ashamed of it... But there was a large part of me that was still embarrassed.

When we stepped into the hall where she had us store our bags, she turned to me and spoke honestly. "I want you to leave class."

"Oh." My eyes went wide, feeling my chest squeeze in pain.

"Not because of the reason you're assuming," she explained softly, "rather the opposite. I want you to go on a walk through the forest. Get some fresh air and try to connect to that part of you. Sometimes being in a confined space, despite my attempt to open up the classroom, can make your animal shy away."

I suppose that made sense.

Nodding in understanding, I went to my locker and grabbed my bag, offering her an embarrassed look. "Sorry about all of this."

"Do not ever apologize for who you are," Ms. Stagshot insisted, her face serious, before she smiled again. "Now go on."

Offering a nod, trying to not deflate completely while around her, I walked down the hall. I went to text Gage to let him know, only to realize that not only was I not supposed to have a cell phone, but the only one I did have was back at the dorms. I hadn't even charged it last night after he'd given it to me.

I wasn't very worried though—I had no doubt he would be able to find me. In fact, all three of them seemed rather skilled at it, so I decided to make my way towards the forested path that would take me to the dorms.

Letting out a small yawn, I realized it was nearly lunch time. My stomach tightened uncomfortably in hunger, and that horrible 'afternoon slump' hit me despite the crisp air that rustled through the trees. The climate here was like a permanently chilled sunny autumn afternoon. It was freaking amazing. But I knew I wouldn't last out here for long, especially with how hungry I was, so I quickly made my way back towards the dorms.

Around five minutes later, I came across a diversion in the path I hadn't noticed before, and while I knew the main one would lead to the dorms, I found myself curious to take the other. I walked casually down the path and froze only when I came to a lake and saw a tall muscular man sitting against one of the rocks. Instantly I felt concern. His entire body was tense, and his hand clutched his auburn hair in frustration.

"Hey there," I offered loudly.

His head snapped over, and his gaze felt familiar but I wasn't sure why.

I offered a friendly smile as I walked towards him. "Mind if I join you?"

"Feel free," he muttered. "I don't own the lake."

Something about that was amusing, but I could tell he was in a serious mood, so I sat down, not making a joke about his phrasing. Inhaling, I realized that his scent was also familiar, and...

"You were the wolf from earlier!" I perked up.

He grunted in affirmation and ran a hand over his face. "And you're the girl living with the dragons."

"Yes." I nodded.

"Shouldn't you be in class? You're in your first year, right?"

"I was dismissed from class," I murmured, feeling a comfortable, friendly energy fill the space around us as I decided to put a small modicum of trust in the man. "It was about connecting with your animal counterpart, and I...I haven't shifted. So she sent me out here."

"Never?" The guy asked, surprise evident on his face.

"Ever." I sighed but then shook off the emotions associated with that. "What about you? Both times I've seen you, you've been in the forest. What gives?"

He smirked. "You have no idea who I am."

"Should I?" I asked seriously, wincing slightly in embarrassment.

"Nah," he mused. "Name is Fletcher."

"Nice to meet you. I'm Bexley, but you can call me Bex."

"Yes, everyone knows who you are for sure." He chuckled and then sighed, his amusement dipping. "And to answer your question, I am avoiding a situation of my own. Or at least trying to think it out before totally fucking it up."

"What's wrong?"

Examining my face, he nodded and decided to trust me. "I'm a wolf, so I am expected to have a wolf mate. It's how it's been for generations. More so, my brother, who took his place here as a professor rather than the head of the family, also should have a wolf mate. In fact, both of us should have *different* wolf mates...but we don't. We don't at all. Our mate is the same person, and I have no idea what to do about it."

I frowned. "Do shifters ever share mates? And if you know who your mate is, I'm assuming they aren't a wolf shifter? Does that really matter? Aren't mate bonds supposed to transcend stuff like that?"

"Do shifters ever share mates?" He offered me a perplexed look. "How much do you know about shifters and their mates, Bex?"

"Not a ton," I admitted. I should have, but somehow the element of 'mating' had largely been left out of my education. At the time I hadn't minded because I did *not* want to talk about that with my tutor, but now it felt embarrassing. Could I be any less of a shifter? I mean, seriously.

He hummed in thought before answering my original question. "Yes they do, but that isn't really the problem. The problem is that my brother and I sharing a mate is difficult when his life is here, and in two years, mine won't be. As for my mate not being a wolf... You wouldn't be wrong, if my family wasn't a bunch of purist assholes."

Oh.

Before I could say anything, I heard someone shout from afar, something that sounded a lot like my name. Fletcher stood up and tossed me a grin. "That would be my cue to leave before I get my head ripped off. Until next time, Bex." Then he shifted in a violent explosion of sprouting fur and cracking bones and was gone, making my eyes widen at his sprinting form.

Fates, that made me jealous! I craved to be able to do that.

"Bex!" Breaker's voice called.

"Her scent is this way—" Jagger's words were cut off as I turned my head to see both of them paused at the entrance of the clearing, staring at me with a mixture of dark emotions, the most prominent one panic.

"What's wrong?" I demanded, standing up and looking at both of them in concern. "Seriously, you both look so worried."

"You disappeared from class," Breaker explained, walking forward. Jagger was still standing there and looking around the clearing, his eyes flashing silver so brightly that I could see it all the way from over here.

"It smells like a wolf," he rumbled, his voice so unlike his normal smooth tone.

I had a feeling I wasn't supposed to directly mention Fletcher, so I offered, "I did see a wolf running through here earlier." That wasn't a lie, either! I had.

"Let's get you back in the dorm," Breaker grunted. I let out a squeak as his hands grabbed my waist and picked me up easily, a giggle following. When he put me down on the path, Jagger cupped my jaw and looked over me with concern.

"Are you okay?"

"Promise I am," I assured.

"Why did you leave class?" Breaker asked as we started walking towards the dorms.

How did I explain that to them? I suppose with the truth, although somehow it felt far more humiliating when telling the two of them. I think it was because I didn't want them to view me as weak or incapable of being here at the academy.

"It was about understanding your animal counter-part, and since I haven't shifted, she told me to take a walk to get some fresh air," I said, my gaze firmly on my feet. Both of them were silent at that, and I let out an exhale. "It's fine, really. I get she's trying to be helpful, and I know I shouldn't let anyone make me feel like crap about not shifting—heck, no one has purposefully been cruel—but there is a part of me that's embarrassed. A part of me that doubts why I'm here. I'm sure people talk and wonder why. I'm positive that they say it's because of the Bronzehearts... It's just a lot at once, you know?"

"We know," Jagger admitted quietly. "You're going to get settled, Bex. It might just take a minute. Maybe this is a good time to figure out this shifting thing."

When we got into the elevator, I turned to both of them. "I've tried. Fates, I have tried to the point of my head hurting and passing out... But there just is nothing there. Sometimes I wonder if I am even a shifter."

"You are a shifter," Breaker insisted. "I can tell you that for fact."

The expressions on their faces told me they believed that, believed me. I just hoped I could prove they were right at some point.

Chapter 14

Bexley

"I'm going to the party tonight," I explained as all three dragons stood near the doorway of my bathroom, while I leaned over the vanity, applying eyeliner.

I was almost ready, and right on time—it was getting late. I may have waited to bring it up to them until the last minute, mainly because I had guessed how they would react. I was starting to realize that, a lot like Gage, there was a part of me that seemed to understand these men instinctively.

That part of me knew they wouldn't love the idea of me going to a party.

"The what?" Jagger demanded, staring at me like I had lost my mind.

To be fair, this was probably a bit surprising to him

since he'd been buried in his dorm doing a project for the past few hours and had come back minutes ago, while I curled my hair. I briefly looked over my outfit, glad I decided to do a somewhat warm weather ensemble tonight, my black jeans tight against my legs and paired with a loose spring green half-top that matched my sandals. I knew I would be cold going to the party, but I was pretty sure the demon sector was far warmer than the others, so it would be worth it.

"The party—the big start of the year party," I explained, stepping back and looking over myself, nodding in approval before heading towards the door. Unfortunately, three large bodies blocked my exit from the bathroom.

"You aren't going to that," Gage rumbled. "That party is always a shit show."

"So you've been?"

Gage's jaw clenched as I tried to appeal to his sense of reason. "I want to experience everything here. I am going to go, even if just for a little bit. I already promised Rachel." I wasn't one to break a promise.

"I have to speak with one of my teammates," Gage said, seemingly stressed at that concept.

Ah, yes, the violent sport they played in the shifter sector. What had they called it again? Rugby? Something like that... I just knew it had come from the humans and it was particularly dangerous. Apparently, much to my surprise, Gage was a huge member of the team, a captain. Once again, I was left feeling like there was too much about him that I didn't know. I didn't like that at all.

I would just have to devote my time to learning even more about him.

"I can go by myself, it will be totally fine. Rachel will be there," I explained.

"Not without one of us," Jagger said sternly. "Someone needs to watch you."

I shook my head before saying, "I really want to go, but I don't need someone to watch me. Especially if you're busy—"

"I'll take her," Breaker rumbled. "Both of you have other places to be."

While I loved the idea of going with them, the way they were discussing it bothered me a bit...

I think it was because it sounded like they were discussing me like I was a responsibility. A job. Like I needed to be babysat. I didn't argue though, slipping past and going to grab a light jacket from my closet. I could hear them bickering, and I felt my body continue to tense.

"Seriously, guys! I can go by myself!" I shouted as I shifted through the hangers, deciding which jacket to wear. I was met by silence, so I added, "I don't like the idea of being a responsibility."

Once again, nothing.

Finally ready, I slipped past them, all of them staring at me in confusion, and went to the elevator. Breaker cursed and appeared right behind me, wrapping an arm around my waist. "Where are you going, *mo chuisle?*"

"The party," I offered with a bit of sass.

"Say goodbye to the others," he commanded softly.

I turned to look at the two of them, and I could see Gage looked frustrated and Jagger concerned. Muttering under my breath, I approached Gage and wrapped my arms around him, feeling annoyed but not knowing how to express why.

"Get some rest after your sports thing," I suggested. I felt like 'sports thing' wasn't the right way to refer to it, but I had never been to a sporting event, let alone a rugby match. That would need to change soon, especially since Gage clearly put so much effort into it. He looked exhausted already from the day, something that he would no doubt deny if asked.

I turned towards Jagger and gave him a hug as well, his body stiff at first until his arms tightened around me. I gave a happy sigh, feeling slightly better about the situation but still upset as I approached the elevator.

Breaker wrapped an arm around me as we stepped into it.

"You really don't have to come, I know you're busy," I offered as the doors closed, wrapping us in silence.

"Not with anything that's more important than your safety," Breaker leveled. "If you think I'm letting you go to that party alone, then you don't realize how valuable you are to me."

Valuable? Well...I liked that a bit more.

"I don't like feeling like a job," I mumbled my insecurity as his eyes darkened.

"You are a responsibility. One I take very seriously."

My chest ached acutely, but instead of saying anything, I tucked my hands in my pockets and walked out of the elevator. He grunted and followed, seeming to not know what to say, and honestly, I had no idea how to explain to him why his words bothered me. When Gage was protective over my safety, it didn't bother me because I knew there was more between us than just that. There was a friendship. But Breaker and Jagger were new to me, and the idea of them viewing me as a responsibility, a burden, really bothered me.

I knew it wasn't a reflection of them as much as myself. I never admitted it, but my situation and history bred some very specific insecurities, mainly that I was a burden to the Bronzehearts. That's why I always tried to never be too much of a problem in any way, why I always did what I was supposed to. They had given me everything, and I didn't want them to ever regret that.

I loved spending time with Breaker and Jagger, a feeling that had only intensified by spending time together after we'd returned back to the dorms. But now I was worried about them regretting meeting me, that they would start to view me as a hassle to deal with. I didn't want that; I wanted them to enjoy spending time with me as much as I loved being around them.

"Bex."

Breaker's voice pulled me from my thoughts as I realized he'd caught up to me. I looked around, finding that I'd been so buried in my thoughts that I'd walked all the way to the path leading out of the sector, the gate looming in the distance ahead, without even realizing it. I swallowed down my insecurities and offered him a tense smile, hoping he wouldn't question where my head had gone.

"Sorry, zoned out," I explained.

"What's going on?" he asked with a knowing look.

As we pushed through the gate, I shook my head. "Nothing, really."

"*Mo chuisle.*" His voice was far more serious as we entered the center pavilion. "Maybe we should head back—"

"No. I *want* to go. This is a good idea." Especially so I could get out of my head a bit instead of overthinking my emotions for hours at a time. "But if you don't want to go, I really do understand." It was far quieter at this time of night, and rather beautiful, but I couldn't focus on that. Instead, I looked back at him, trying to get a bit of distance before finally giving him an out.

"Breaker, there is no reason to follow me," I explained, trying to sound relaxed about it and relieving him of his duties. "I already told Gage where I'd be at. I really don't need a babysitter."

I expected him to retort, but instead he pulled me to a hard stop, causing my attention to follow where he was looking over my head. *Crap*, I hadn't realized people were around to see our little show.

"Oh, hey!"

Way to play it cool, Bex. Very, very cool.

Instantly, I was categorizing the group of six. I wasn't positive how I knew it—maybe because of the magic I could feel coming off them—but I had a feeling they were witches. There was also a really dark edge to them, surrounding them like a mass of power that pulsed, making something defensive stir in my chest. It wasn't their fault, though. I think it came natural to them, so I still wanted to be friendly.

"Breaker," the man in the center of the group

offered in greeting, his arm tightening around the only woman with them.

As intimidating as the men in the group came across, my attention was fully on the woman with them, because I was fairly positive she was far more dangerous. She was also drop-dead gorgeous, with the most unusual blue hair and silver eyes. It was extremely striking, and while she looked currently relaxed, I had a feeling that she could snap out of that easily. Much like with Rachel, I found myself wanting to be her friend.

I suppose I had never had girlfriends before. I mean Ms. Payne and Celine were wonderful, but I'd never been friends with girls my own age. It was difficult to do so when I knew most of them liked Gage.

Something that bothered me for far more than one reason.

"Grim," Breaker replied and then nodded towards the rest in greeting. "You guys coming back from the party?"

"Yes." The girl nodded, directing her attention towards me, a smile lighting up her face. "It's super fun, and I wish I could go back."

I had a feeling that she was a bit tipsy, her face flushed, but she also looked like she meant it...which meant I had to go. Plus, I couldn't leave my friend hanging.

"See!" I looked up at Breaker, a slight almost frustrated growl in my voice that seemed to make his eyes jump in amusement. "I have to go, she said it was 'super fun.'"

I had no doubt that if Breaker didn't think this was a good idea, he could drag me right back to the dorm, and I really didn't want that to happen.

"Bexley..." He offered me a slight warning look. Instead of scaring me to any extent, it had my center clenching and heat flashing over me.

"Bex," I nitpicked, scowling slightly, as he smirked.

I looked back at the girl, deciding I needed to take direct action to ensure I made it to the party. "It was wonderful to meet you, but I am going to that party—"

I was speed walking away from the conversation before Breaker could stop me, but I felt him hot on my tail. I reached the demon sector gate and slipped through... Right before Breaker looped a large arm around my waist and tugged me against him.

I let out a small groan of defeat. His chuckle had me scowling, but before I could get too upset, my back hit a tree and I realized we were in the shadows, out of range of all the students gathering nearby. I didn't even have a chance to look at the party or see what it was like because everything was blocked out by his frame.

I found I loved it more than I could have even expected.

"What are we doing?" I asked, trying to offer him a pointed look but failing as my cheeks heated at the intensity in his gaze.

"You and I clearly need to talk," Breaker rumbled. "You are my responsibility, Bex, and I love it—"

"But I have no reason to be your responsibility," I interrupted. He cupped my jaw and ran a thumb over my lips, effectively silencing me.

He continued, ignoring my statement. "I don't know why you view that as a bad thing, but being my responsibility means that I will always look out for you, always take care of you, because I care about you, Bexley. I want to do this. I need to do this."

Oh.

I stared at him wide-eyed, his declaration catching me off guard as I struggled to find what to say. So I offered the only thing I could come up with. "It's Bex."

I really was horrible at this, fates. To be fair, it had been a very long day!

Breaker kept looking at me intently, practically demanding a real response. I sighed. "I just...I never want to feel like a burden to anyone, Breaker. Of course the Bronzehearts never made me feel that way, but they took me off the streets. They didn't have to take care of me, but they did. I always worry they may end up regretting that. I don't want anyone to ever feel like I'm a job."

"Even if you were a job, you would be an amazing one." He smoothed a strand of my hair back gently. "But you are my responsibility. Don't take that away from me."

"Alright," I conceded. I wanted to ask him why again, but I had a feeling he wouldn't answer. Not yet, anyway.

"Now, this party," he began, looking to the side where the other students were. "We can stay, but only while it's safe. Those witches aren't exactly the type of company that promises this will be a safe party."

I wanted to ask how he knew them, but I figured it wasn't the time. Especially if it reminded him of how unsafe and dangerous they were.

"I've got you by my side," I pointed out, trying to lighten the mood. "You're like my body guard." My massive, muscular body guard who I was totally attracted to.

Breaker let out a laugh, seeming to find that funny as he led me forward and away from the trees. I came to a stop, a smile lighting up my face when I saw where everyone was heading.

"Holy crap." *This was beyond cool.*

Shrugging off my jacket, Breaker released a rumble

but took it. I knew he realized how hot it was here—I mean, it was impossible not to notice—and I was really happy with my outfit choice.

"Fates, you are beautiful." Breaker exhaled sharply as if he was in pain. I looked up at him in concern, only to realize he was looking at me with heat again, the same as when we were in bed together.

"Thank you," I murmured, loving how he intertwined our fingers as we followed a group of students towards the mountain range with a forest edging the perimeter.

I was nearly bouncing with excitement as the music and magic of everyone at the party hit me, causing me to almost feel as if I was feeding off of it. *It was amazing.* All different kinds of students celebrating in one place. I couldn't help but look around at everyone, noticing how colorful and different everyone seemed to be.

When Breaker led me towards a bar that was situated between two massive trees, lit up with small hovering lights that seemed to blink in and out of existence, I leaned up into his ear. "I need to try to find my friend."

"Let's get you something light to drink so no one offers you anything," he suggested. "If you have a drink in your hand, no one will try to give you another. Usually."

I nodded, impressed by his party knowledge as he ordered me a 'light ale.' Honestly, I wasn't a huge drinker. Outside of a champagne toast, I didn't have much experience with alcohol, but I was more than willing to give ale a chance.

"What's an ale?" I asked curiously as he led me towards the far side of the dance floor. I took the glass bottle from him and took a sip, the explosion of apples and a slight berry taste hitting my tongue.

I let out a hum of pleasure as I smiled up at him. "This is better than champagne for sure."

He chuckled softly. "Good, I'm glad. Now, let's try to find your friend."

I nodded, looking around, wishing that I was just a bit taller so I could see over everyone's massive height... I saw a flash of pink hair and instantly smiled.

"There she is!" I pointed towards a group of girls that seemed to be nervous to go onto the dance floor. I strode towards Rachel, and she suddenly looked up and offered me a big grin, waving and practically bouncing on her toes.

"Hey you," I greeted, hugging her. The other girls gawked at me, not saying anything. I felt momentarily awkward, trying to offer them small smiles.

"Hey!" Rachel chirped, far more spirited than earlier. "I am so glad you came! These are my dorm mates—Becca, Mimi, and Ashley. They're sophomores and are all deer shifters."

"Wonderful to meet you," I said, smiling.

"Don't worry, she's super nice," Rachel assured her friends before turning back to me. "They are scared of your dragon."

Your dragon. *My dragon.* I loved that.

I turned towards Breaker and smiled up at him. "You're scaring them. I don't think you're scary, but they do because you're a dragon."

He flashed me a dangerous smile. "Sorry, *mo chuisle,* I'm not going anywhere. But if you want to go on the dance floor, I will stay here."

"Oh, that's a great idea!" I tugged on Rachel's hand to bring her to the dance floor, hoping that this would be the key to making the others realize I wasn't nearly as intimidating as they believed. Especially since you couldn't be scared of someone when they were as horrible of a dancer as myself. I freely admitted that—in fact, it was a bit of a joke between Gage's mom and me. The one time she had suggested I take ballet lessons... Well, it failed horribly. Still, that didn't stop me from having fun with Rachel. We kept to ourselves despite the large mass on the dance floor, and I slowly convinced the three others to join us. Within thirty minutes I had finished my ale, and the five of us girls were dancing as Breaker watched from the side, his eyes completely focused on me.

I could see that level of heat there, and I was starting to wonder if maybe Breaker felt not just a physical connection to me but something stronger. I didn't have a lot of experience with any of this, but something about the way he claimed me as his 'responsibility' felt different. It felt more possessive.

After nearly an hour, I realized I didn't want the night to come to an end. In fact, I wanted to pull Breaker onto the dance floor with me...

Then chaos broke out.

I let out a surprised sound as I was shoved violently to the side by someone knocking into me. I nearly fell on top of Rachel, but luckily Breaker caught me as something crashed around us, followed by yelling that filled the air. Breaker placed me near the tree line as my friends left the dance floor, looking nearly as shocked as myself. I looked up at Breaker to see how stressed he suddenly appeared.

"Stay here with the girls; I have to break this up. Stupid fucking wolves." Breaker was gone as a full-fledged brawl broke out on the dance floor.

"That's nice of him," a calm, almost raspy female voice pulled my attention to the edge of the tree line. I blinked, realizing that there was a woman standing there. She had blended into the background, in part because of her dark clothes, but now that I was looking at her, I realized she had silver hair that seemed to float around her and crimson eyes. It was so unique, it caught me off guard for a minute before catching up to the moment.

"What?" I asked curiously.

"Your dragon, going to break that up," she explained. "I was sort of hoping it would get more violent before someone stepped in."

The expression on her face was filled with tension despite her doing her best to hide it. I stepped slightly closer to talk to her, the noise growing louder around us. In her hand was some type of short glass with dark liquid. How she managed to look classy at a party like this was extremely impressive.

"Why?" I asked,

"It's entertaining," she offered and flashed me a smile, making my eyes widen. *She had fangs!* Hadn't I just been saying that I wanted to meet a vampire?

"You're a vampire," I said in awe, needing confirmation.

A dark shadow passed her face before she let out a dry laugh. "Yeah... I guess I am."

I frowned, tilting my head. "You guess?"

"Doesn't matter," she dismissed as she flicked her

long hair over her shoulders. With a raise of her eyebrow, she muttered, "Not quite used to admitting that yet."

I felt like it did matter, but I also felt wrong pushing it when I barely knew her.

"I'm Bexley," I said, offering a small smile. "But you can call me Bex."

Her eyes glanced over my body, as if summing me up before offering a soft smile. "Alina," she returned and then tilted her head. "You're a shifter?"

"Yes..." I hesitated. "Sort of?" Now I sounded like the unsure one.

"Sort of?" She mused before taking a sip of her drink and scanning the crowd in front of us. It seemed like she was vigilantly watching the event despite portraying a calm demeanor. As if she was prepared for an attack at any moment.

"I have never shifted," I admitted. I think the more I said it, the less embarrassed I felt... Or at least that was what I was telling myself.

Alina offered a hum of amusement. "Well, it seems that neither of us fit in with our people."

"Yeah, you're right." I knew that was for sure the case with me.

Suddenly, Alina's gaze went over my shoulder. "It was nice to meet you, Bex. I am going to head out. It seems you may be as well. I hope we cross paths again soon. If you ever find yourself in my sector, just ask for the crazy bitch. They'll point you in my direction."

Crazy bitch? She didn't seem crazy or like a bitch to me, but I knew it wasn't my place to contradict that.

"And if you come to the shifter sector, just ask for the shifter that doesn't shift and lives with dragons," I offered, giving a small smile that she matched. A warm thread of friendship filled the space, the moment interrupted by someone calling my name.

I frowned, looking over my shoulder, not seeing anything besides the chaotic crowd, and when I looked back she was gone. How the heck had she done that? I couldn't imagine being able to move that fast. I was completely jealous.

"Time to go." Breaker's voice was filled with tension, and I could tell he was legitimately stressed by what was going on.

"Okay," I agreed, feeling a wave of exhaustion from the day. I looked at Rachel and her roommates, who were staring at us with concern. I had a feeling they weren't feeling the party anymore either. "We are heading out, you want to join us?"

"Yes please." Rachel nodded.

As we walked through the party, keeping to the edges, Breaker made sure to shield me from anyone while still keeping tabs on my friends to make sure they made it out without incident. I knew he didn't need to do that, so it was really sweet of him to keep their safety in mind. By the time we approached the gate, everyone seemed far more relaxed and in better spirits.

As we entered the pavilion, my new friends went ahead, wishing me goodnight as Breaker wrapped me in his body heat. I looked at the administration building as he stopped to put my jacket back around my shoulders, the clang of the shifter sector gate closing echoing in the tepid night air.

Loudly.

"Does the school know about the party?" I asked curiously.

"Yes." He chuckled.

"And they let it happen anyway?"

"I assume they figure it's better to let the students do small things, like a party, that they can control rather than something larger."

It made sense to me.

I turned into him and tilted my head back. "Thanks for coming with me tonight. I know it started off a bit rocky, but I really appreciate it."

Breaker clasped my jaw with one large hand, looking over my expression. "Always, Bex. Whenever you need to go somewhere, just ask me. I always want to make sure you're safe."

I swallowed, feeling a blush hit my cheek at the intensity and sincerity of his tone.

Suddenly, boldness striking me, I went up on my toes and slammed my lips against his. A groan rumbled from his throat as his large fingers strung through my hair and held me against him. I whimpered as I parted my lips, allowing him to invade my mouth, his kiss both sweet and almost toxic. I let out a shaky breath when he finally pulled back and blinked, feeling dazed.

"Damn."

Pride flashed in his gaze. "I want that look on your face forever."

Somehow, someway, I had no doubt he could do exactly that. *Forever*.

Chapter 15

Jagger Silvershade

I had yet to sleep.

No, instead I had sat on the couch all night, waiting for my little treasure to wake up. I knew it was ridiculous—she obviously wasn't going anywhere —but I was plagued by previous memories, and I was obsessed with wanting to know that she was in fact here, finally. That I wouldn't wake up and realize that we were back to never being able to see her, living off of scraps that Cage was able to smuggle to us about her.

I ran a hand through my hair while staring up at the ceiling in thought, the fire crackling as the early morning light filled her dorm with a stunning glow. I bet she would look beautiful spread out in her bed. Her bed that I desperately wanted to be in. When she had come back from that party, I'd been so relieved that I'd nearly stolen her away from Gage and Breaker, both wanting her attention, so that I could hold her.

I wasn't sure I deserved that though.

In fact, after nearly knocking her unconscious by bringing up shit I shouldn't have, I wasn't positive I deserved anything related to Bexley. *The woman I was supposed to be keeping safe for the rest of my life.* Although, I could at least partly blame Gage for my fuck-up. He'd told us that certain things could trigger Bexley passing out, but he'd never told us how sensitive she was. I swallowed, deciding to get up and make some coffee to get my mind off of everything I was doing wrong.

There had been so many times in my life when I had wanted to storm into the Bronzeheart estate and demand her back. Not just physically, although I would have loved to steal her like the treasure she so clearly was, but demand that she come back to me mentally, emotionally. Demand that she remember everything we'd been through.

How was it fair that the one thing that could fix all of this—the truth—would literally physically damage her? I put my forehead against the kitchen cabinets as I turned on the coffee maker.

I'd made sure to get peppermint creamer and sugar for her dorm, so I was hoping that she would love waking up to a large mug of coffee already ready for her. I also was secretly hoping that the smell of it would wake her up. I knew she needed sleep, but I also found myself selfishly wanting alone time with her.

I wasn't wrong about my prediction though, and about five minutes later, the scent had a very sleepy, gorgeous Bexley stumbling from her room. I nearly groaned. This woman was going to kill me. How she managed to be unintentionally sexy and cute was something I'd never understand.

Seriously, her golden hair was messy and hung around her shoulders, she had a sleep mask pushed up on her forehead, and she was wearing silky cream-colored pajamas that made her skin look like it was glowing. Her sleepy gaze found mine, and she offered me a small, shy smile that nearly had me falling to my knees. The control this woman had over me was absolutely unreal.

"Wow, you look handsome today," she murmured and then blushed. "Oh my fates, did I say that out loud?"

I barked out a laugh, feeling instantly energized by her appreciation, as I pulled down a mug for her. I knew from Gage that she liked a specific brand of coffee mugs that were extra large, and I'd stocked this place up with them. Today it was a lavender one that had an uplifting phrase scripted on the front. I poured her some coffee, adding creamer and sugar as she sat down at the island.

"How are you feeling after last night?" I asked. I didn't think she had enough to drink to have a hangover, but I hadn't considered getting her pain medicine or water instead of coffee. Shit.

"Good." She smiled brightly. "That was the first time I went to a party outside of formal events." Her eyes filled with confusion for a minute. "Which reminds me, why do the clans never have events together? I wish I had met Breaker and you before now."

Oh, but she had. I tried to figure out the best way to explain that to her without causing her any physical distress.

"There was a dispute about eight years ago that caused some major problems—lots of suspicion and mistrust—and because of that, our families are not on friendly terms," I admitted before pouring myself a cup of coffee.

Her eyes turned thoughtful. "But you three are friends."

"Yes, we have a united cause though, besides being best friends," I offered quietly.

"I like that. Maybe...maybe during the summer and stuff, you guys can come and visit the Bronzeheart estate. I bet I could convince Celine it's a good idea."

I had no doubt that Bexley was capable of that, but the only place she would be staying this summer was somewhere all three of us could reach her. I finally had her back, and I wasn't giving her up again. I just couldn't say that to her. Not yet. The corners of my mouth turned down as I thought about the last time I'd seen her before *everything* happened.

"This is stupid," Gage growled. "We should let her decide."

I didn't disagree, but I also didn't like the idea of Bexley deciding who she wanted to be friends with more. Who she wanted to spend more time with. What if she didn't pick me? Plus, why couldn't she split her time? We were all friends anyway.

I wasn't positive what had gotten into Breaker and Gage lately, but they seemed determined on making our friend choose.

"Or she shouldn't," I grumbled, although I'd mostly given up on that. They didn't care for my suggestion, I knew it.

"She has to," Breaker argued. "You can't have multiple best friends."

Which was the stupidest logic I'd ever heard since the three of us were best friends...but I think I knew that this wasn't just about being friends. At least not just being friends with Bexley. Lately all I could think about was how pretty my friend was—the prettiest girl I'd ever met—and I knew that my friends saw it too.

Dragons liked pretty things, so I didn't blame them for wanting to keep her to themselves...but we had to share. I knew that; it was almost instinctively a fact.

Before we could argue any more, a small sob sounded from inside the house. We were currently on a long weekend at the Bronzeheart estate, and I never moved as fast as I did upon hearing that cry.

When I came into the house, I found Bexley crying on a bench, her hands covering her face as she tried to muffle the sound. I didn't hesitate to pick her up, positioning her on my lap, as I heard Gage demand to know what was wrong.

Breaker was staring at her in concern. I had a feeling that he was thinking about what we would do if someone had hurt her, and instantly an anger and violence I didn't know I had inside of me reared up.

"You're making me choose, you're going to make me pick a friend," she cried into my neck. "I don't want to pick between you guys."

Oh.

We were the ones who had hurt her.

No. That wasn't right.

"You don't have to," I promised her. She sniffled, her crying pausing as she looked up at me with large worried eyes, clearly not believing me.

"I heard you guys talking about—"

"We were being stupid," I soothed. "You don't have to do anything you don't want to, Bex." Examining her face, I watched as she let out a shaky breath and hugged me again. I offered both Gage and Breaker a hard look, and they looked more conflicted than before.

I didn't care what it would take, I would not hurt her.

"Or not." Bex's soft voice pulled me out of my reverie. "You don't have to visit, of course." I could see sadness in her gaze, and I realized I'd been caught in my memory for too long. I walked around the island and cupped her jaw with my fingers, trying to suppress the urge to kiss her. I wanted to. Fuck, did I want to, and unfortunately, I didn't have the patience of Gage.

I did, however, have a level of self-preservation, and I knew that if I kissed Bexley, I would be done for. I would give her anything and everything she wanted, even if she asked for something that could potentially hurt her.

"I would love to see you, no matter where you are," I

assured her and then looked down at her lips. "I think you're going to find it hard to get rid of us, little treasure."

"And what if I like that?" Her words were quiet, as if she was unsure if she should say them out loud.

I inhaled sharply, trying to ignore my dragon who wanted to break loose of the chains I bound him under. "All the better, but I don't think you could stop us following you around, even if you tried."

Just like before.

Bex drew in her bottom lip thoughtfully as her cheeks flushed pink. "Why do I like that so much?"

Because she knew the truth. A part of her knew the truth.

"Jagger?" Her voice was suddenly quieter, her eyes flicking down to my lips.

"Yeah, little treasure?"

"I want to kiss you."

Sweet fates, I had never heard more beautiful words. I met her heated gaze, and instead of making her take the first move, I decided to say 'fuck it' and kiss her like I'd been wanting to since Sunday.

Hell, since long before that.

Bending down to reach her, my lips hovered over hers as a small tremble ran over her skin and her desire filled the air. I wanted this moment burned into my subconscious forever. I never wanted to forget when I claimed her lips.

I let out a throaty rumble before melting our lips together. Instantly, the sweet, natural scent of rain on her skin filled the space, mixing with her desire, and I tried to keep control of my dragon. My dragon that was roaring in my chest violently to claim her, and not just her mouth. My dragon that was no doubt causing my eyes to turn silver. When I pulled back, holding her face captive, I noticed that her eyes were starting to bleed black, a clear sign of her shifted side.

It was so gorgeous, the inky surface filled with gold specs, that I was snared in her trap, completely mesmerized. I wanted to tell her about it, to show her the proof of what she was... But I couldn't. I couldn't tell her that she was not only a shifter but something far more amazing.

I could feel my beast trying to connect with her own creature as I dipped my lips back to hers. I intended it to be another gentle kiss, almost exploratory in nature... Then she nipped my bottom lip.

My dragon broke out before I could stop him.

I had Bex flat on her back on the softest surface nearby in a second flat, her wrists captured in my hands as I tasted the blood between us. Her little whimpers and moans against my mouth only fueled me more, and

I rocked against her, never having been this hard before.

"Jagger." She gasped as I kissed down her jaw, and my teeth began to pulse as I bypassed the part of her neck that I desperately wanted to mark.

I couldn't. I wanted to, more than anything, but I couldn't. I had to draw the line somewhere, right?

Fuck, my head was so damn fuzzy with need, and when her hands began to explore along my chest, I found myself sucking hard on the delicate skin. She jolted, moaning out my name, as I realized with pleasure that she'd come.

My little treasure had come from rubbing against me, and when I pulled back to look at her, her face was flushed and eyes completely black. I pressed my forehead to hers and let out a deep rumble, knowing she would probably be upset about the mark I left on her neck. And if she wasn't... Well, Breaker and especially Gage would be.

Honestly, it was fucking worth it. I could deal with them.

"Fuck," I murmured, feeling dazed. "I am never going to be able to focus again when I look at your lips."

"That was amazing," she whispered. "I've never....I mean...I've never..." Her face was flushed, as if she wasn't sure how to say what she meant. I blinked, feeling a surge of pride at the realization of what she was trying to communicate. I let out a low growl, brushing her lips.

"Come? Was that the first time you've come, little treasure?"

"Yes," she admitted breathlessly.

I groaned and slipped my fingers down, coasting over her sleep shorts where the silk was damp with her need. "Do you ever touch yourself, Bex?" Because I wanted to see that so fucking much.

"Sometimes," she murmured, "but I've never been able to... Well, you know."

"Come," I rumbled. "That's because you need me. I'll always make sure you feel good, little treasure."

Bex nodded, looking breathless and surprised at my words—which would make two of us. I had no idea where this side of me was coming from.

Actually, that wasn't true. I did know. I knew it had always been there. I may have been the quietest out of the three of us, but I had always known what I'd wanted from Bex. When it was just the two of us, I was in charge. It was just the natural dynamic for us.

Now I just needed her to realize it... Or maybe she already did. I loved the way she melted under my touch; it made me feel like a goddamn king.

"Jagger!" A booming voice had me groaning as I sat back, not even trying to hide how hard I was.

I nodded towards Bex's bathroom. "Go get ready for the day, Bex. I have to handle something—*fuck*." I groaned as Gage ripped me away from her and managed to toss me into the wall, the entire place shuddering as something crashed to the floor.

Fuck, that had hurt.

I straightened up immediately, seeing that he was fucking livid, but I found I didn't care. He got to spend every goddamn day with her since everything had happened. If I wanted to kiss her, I would. I wouldn't mark her until she knew the truth, I'd always agreed to that, but if she wanted me to kiss her? I would fucking kiss her.

"You're a bastard," Gage snarled, holding her captive against him. I knew he didn't mean that, and I could tell his dragon was riding him hard, but I also wasn't going to let him get away with being an ass.

"You're jealous," I spit out. "I'm not doing this with you, Gage."

I wouldn't fight with him, not over her.

"You are taking advantage of her because of the—"

"Stop!" Bex pulled out of his arms and narrowed her eyes at him. "Stop it, Gage, seriously. I wanted him to kiss me," she fumed, pointing to her own chest violently.

"*I* wanted that. He wasn't taking advantage of me. I told him I wanted to kiss him."

Gage inhaled sharply, looking frustrated and jealous. "Bex, you don't understand."

"Don't understand what?" she asked, throwing out her hands in exasperation. "What I want? I may have been sheltered, Gage, but I still know what I want, or who I want."

Did he not hear the sadness in her voice? It was very clear to me that Bex felt strongly for Gage—really fucking strongly, even though she couldn't yet feel the mate bond—but she had accepted that he didn't see her as more than a friend, and this wasn't making it better. I knew he wanted to keep her safe, but she was perfectly capable of making her own choices, and the fact that she was now had him in a tailspin. His world had always been controlled with Bex safely at the center, and I knew my friend had a limited time until he truly lost it.

Gage stormed from the dorm. I rubbed the back of my head where I'd hit it before looking towards Bex, who sat down on the couch, watching him leave.

"Why did he walk out?" she whispered, curling in on herself.

"I think Gage is used to being the only person in your life, and now that he's not, he's upset," I reasoned. I also thought he was a jealous bastard who wanted all of

Bexley's firsts because he knew her the best. Or at least that was how he felt.

"I just feel confused," she murmured.

"Go get ready," I suggested softly. "I will take you to class."

"Okay."

I watched her go, her shoulders sagging in defeat. I narrowed my eyes at Gage's dorm, tempted to give him a piece of my mind, but I would wait until he calmed down. I knew how bad it could get between us.

We may have been friends, but our dragons weren't—especially when it came to her.

Chapter 16

Bexley

By the end of *Hierarchy in Shifter Dominance*, I realized that there was absolutely no way I would be able to focus. It didn't help that Mr. Stillbow, despite seeming very knowledgeable, had the most calming voice on the planet, making me want to put my head down and fall asleep.

I looked around the classroom, realizing that almost everyone seemed in the same position. Even Rachel, who was slowly sipping on her travel mug of coffee, her eyes half closed despite her efforts. Right about now I was wishing that someone sat in front of us just so I could hide behind them and take a small nap.

I hadn't slept very well last night, and then the incident this morning left me feeling...off. Gage and I didn't usually fight, and lately there had been a lot of tension between us. I knew it had to do with my relationship with Breaker and Jagger, one I completely didn't understand but was growing to love. Still, the situation left me feeling uneasy, and I was eager to head home for the day.

It didn't help that it was colder than normal today, so I was wearing a cozy sweater dress and boots that wrapped around my tight-covered legs. I even had put on a jacket that I had positioned over my shoulders. I could have made the choice to cover up my neck, considering the massive hickey on my skin there, but...I hadn't. Something that Jagger had loved despite him not saying so. I could just tell by the amount of times he'd looked at it, and honestly, I hadn't been upset about it. No, instead I had just been upset that I hadn't marked him.

What the heck was that about? Since when did the idea of marking someone, specifically Jagger, become a thing for me?

With a small groan, I finally gave in and closed my eyes, just momentarily. I just needed to close them for a second...

The next thing I knew, Rachel was shaking me awake. "Class is over," she explained.

Thank the fates. I hated to admit it, but the class had been boring. Although, to be fair, it was a simple concept that the class was based around—dragons were the top and shifters that were prey-like animals were the lowest tier.

Done. Easy.

I hated it, but I tried to push past that because I knew it was a necessary class that I had to do well in. Even though it felt like a stab in the gut whenever Mr. Stillbow referred to some shifters as 'weak' openly.

"I am going to take a nap after lunch," I murmured as I stood to walk out of the room, my bag comfortably over my shoulder.

"Let's get out of here—*ow!*" I hissed as a heavy frame hit against me in passing. I reared back as I realized it was Ioan.

He had been glaring at me all class, but I was somewhat hoping he'd stop. It was beyond awkward. I knew he was pissed about yesterday, but he seemed to take it as a personal offense that I didn't want to spend time with him, and if I was to believe my dragons, offended that I didn't want *him*.

Now he had gone out of his way to physically hurt me.

"Did you just hit into her?" Rachel demanded, looking furious.

"She should watch herself," Ioan spat, looking at my neck with disgust. "She doesn't belong here in the first place."

What the heck? I blinked, shaking my head as he strode out and past me.

I swallowed, feeling both hurt by his words, because they were sharp and targeted my direct insecurity, but more than that...my shoulder actually hurt. I rolled it and followed Rachel out, not realizing that she was talking to me until she gently pulled me to a stop with a hand on my forearm.

"You okay?" she asked softly. "You should tell your guys about what he did."

I loved the 'your guys,' but instead of cheering me up, this time I just kept thinking about how worked up they would get when they found out about this.

I knew they would want me to tell them, but even if they threatened him like yesterday, it would probably just make things way worse. There was enough tension as it was; I didn't want to add more.

"Maybe." I sighed. "Let's just get some lunch for now."

Our walk was slow and quiet as we neared the dining hall. I didn't mind the cooler weather, but I preferred to get out of the direct cold wind. I shifted my jacket, and when we reached the dining hall doors, the smell of food instantly made me feel far better.

My stomach clenched, and I didn't pay attention to

the eyes on us because there was only one thing I wanted, and it was... *Breaker?*

I mean, I did want him... I blinked, surprised to find him standing right there, seemingly waiting for me.

Rachel squeezed my arm in passing before saying, "Tell him what happened." Then she was gone, most likely to join her roommates, who were sitting a few tables away.

I offered Breaker a small smile, hoping he hadn't heard, but his once relaxed smile turned concerned as he looked over me. I reached him, and instantly he was pulling out a chair and motioning for me to sit. As I did, he crouched in front of me so we were more eye level, although I still had to look up at him.

"What happened?" His soft demand had my skin breaking out into shivers. Unlike every other shifter I'd met, something about my dragons demanding answers from me made me feel...different.

"Happened? When did something happen?" I was not only distracted by him, but I didn't know if he meant the class thing or the very weird moment between Gage and Jagger today, something he had no doubt been informed about. Both were completely valid, and both were bothering me to a larger extent.

"Bexley, what happened in class?" His voice was a

low rumble. My toes curled, and a flash of heat went over my skin before I registered his words.

"It's Bex," I reminded him. "I don't like Bexley."

I normally hated it—it reminded me of that night when I was so scared... But when he said it, I liked it, which meant he couldn't say it anymore. That made sense, right?

"It's your name," he pointed out, his eyes jumping with amusement.

"And as my name, I don't want you to use it." I poked him in his broad, muscular chest, and his hand came out to grab my wrist in a shockingly fast move. He offered me a smile as hushed whispers broke out around us. My entire body went still as he gently kissed the top of my hand, and I felt my cheeks heat. This man had kissed me, yet somehow these softer, more public, displays of affection had me feeling a high of pleasure at how he was touching me.

"Was that supposed to hurt?" he asked.

No. I would never want to hurt him.

"Maybe." I shrugged, trying to keep it light. "You'll never know. You should always be ready for a possible attack."

"Yeah, *mo chuisle*?" He moved closer and brushed my nose. "Or will it be me attacking you?"

That didn't sound nearly as scary as it should have.

I licked my lips. "That doesn't sound like a bad idea." In fact, it sounded wonderful.

"Not until you tell me what happened in class," he persisted, and I muttered a curse before finally sinking into my chair. I knew I had to tell him.

"Ioan hit into me at the end of class and it hurt my shoulder. Then he said I should watch myself." *There!* Nice, simple... And Breaker did not look happy.

"He did what?" His growl, the way his throat vibrated with a primal noise, had my toes curling as I heard shifters around us literally getting up to leave, the sound of chairs scraping against the floor causing me to jolt. I didn't blame them, he was scary... hot also, but scary was valid.

"Hit my shoulder with his," I clarified.

Breaker's gaze was a pure metallic gold as he examined my right arm and shoulder, somehow knowing that was the injured one. I had no idea what he was thinking, but I could tell he was pissed. Really pissed.

"I need to feed you and then look at your shoulder," he said, looking around and adding, "without all these damn eyes on you."

"Back to the dorm?" I offered. "We have food there."

After the events of the past couple days, I think my dragons were determined to make sure I could stay in my dorm as much as possible, stocking it full of food and anything else I could want. Outside of classes, it was totally working.

After assessing my expression, he nodded and then literally scooped me up in a bridal hold and strode out of the dining hall. I considered fighting him on the whole picking me up thing, but honestly it felt really nice, so I just relaxed into him. My shoulder was still radiating an uncomfortable pain despite being tucked against him, and while I knew Ioan hadn't broken anything, the power he had put behind it had been enough to leave a lasting effect.

Once we were in the elevator, Breaker's speed down the forest path unbelievably fast, he put me down and I shimmied out of my jacket. I offered to take my bag but instead he took my coat, relieving me of holding anything.

Breaker was far quieter than normal as we stepped into my dorm and he placed my stuff down. I didn't argue with him when he put me in front of the fire and got to cooking. In fact, the next thirty or so minutes were spent in silence, and while it was a comfortable one, I was a bit worried about what he was thinking. I could see the wheels turning in his head, and I was worried that he was going to lose his cool.

Or go and find Ioan.

Finally, when he brought me a large bowl of what appeared to be a soup, I ate while he stared at me.

Finally, I decided to finally say something. "It hurts a bit less now."

Breaker's eyes flared pure gold. "Never ever hesitate to tell me if someone hurts you, understand?"

I did. I also had a feeling I'd hurt him by not telling him outright the moment I saw him.

I nodded and put down my bowl, knowing he needed to see the potential injury in order to feel better. I pushed up the very loose sleeves of my sweater dress to show him my perfectly fine... *holy fates,* bruised shoulder. He hissed, looking livid as his eyes flared, and he went over to the kitchen and grabbed some ice.

"It will heal," I promised, not wanting to cause too much of an issue, but I could tell he wasn't listening to me.

Instead he insisted on setting me up on the couch and putting ice on my shoulder, looking over me with concern that didn't match the anger seething under his skin.

"I need to—"

"Don't," I begged. "Don't leave, and don't go find him. He's not worth it."

"He physically hurt you." Breaker's jaw clenched. "That is not acceptable. He can't hurt my fucking m—"

I hissed as pain speared through my temples, my hearing going out. When his hands came on either side of my jaw, I looked up at him and tried to focus, wondering what the hell that had been about.

"What did you say?" I whispered in confusion, my stomach rolling.

"Nothing," Breaker murmured, his gaze filled with so many emotions I couldn't process them. "Close your eyes for a bit, I will stay here till the others come back."

I believed him. I knew he wouldn't leave me, and my eyes fell heavily as I gave into the sleep that had been calling me this entire time.

"I promise I am perfectly fine," I assured them for the four-millionth time. I really did feel much better, even if they didn't believe me. "My shoulder is literally healed!" I pointed out.

Much like Breaker, Gage and Jagger seemed to be worked up, and despite trying to calm them—even offering to teach them knitting, which seemed to lighten up the mood just a tad—they were furious. I knew they wanted to go find Ioan, but I didn't want that. I didn't want any more problems.

In fact, I had been trying to come up with ways to

distract them for some time now, and there wasn't anything I could think of. Well, that wasn't one hundred percent true—there were a few things I could think of, but they were ones that I wasn't bold enough to pull off yet, not with one of them and for sure not all three of them. Well, two I suppose... I knew that Breaker and Jagger would probably be okay with that, but Gage? I still didn't know where I stood with Gage.

My cheeks flushed, knowing where I *wished* I stood with Gage.

"He needs to be taught a lesson." Gage's voice was eerily calm despite how angry he was. "You know that, right? Even if it's not tonight. He can't get away with hurting you."

I think I did know that, but I didn't want to be the cause for violence. The thought made me physically sick to my stomach.

"It doesn't feel right," I explained softly. "I don't want you guys to get in trouble, but more than that, I don't want to be the reason for violence."

"How mad will you be if it happens without your permission? If we hurt him understanding that you weren't okay with it? Or didn't condone it?" Jagger asked bluntly, causing my eyes to widen. I considered his question and found there was a part of me, most likely the shifter side, that liked the idea of them defending my honor, but it was buried within so many parts of me that said this was wrong. I felt very, very undecided on how to proceed.

"I would be upset..." I hesitated. "But I would forgive you."

"I can handle that," Jagger murmured almost to himself.

Gage grunted. "I can't. Cupcake, you have to understand why we need to defend you and make this right."

"But I don't. I get that we all care about each other," I said, trying to uncomplicate it and feeling like that embodied everything. Sort of. "But it was one time. I have a suspicion the more we escalate this, the worse it's going to get." Ioan clearly wasn't the type to let a perceived insult go.

Breaker ran a hand through his hair, looking stressed.

"Besides..." I put down my knitting stuff. I had been in the process of starting a new scarf made of silver, gold, and bronze colored yarn with a metallic sheen to it. I wasn't going to say that it was inspired by my room-mates, but I also wasn't going to say it wasn't. "I want to try shifting tonight."

Well that seemed to surprise them.

"You want to do what?" Gage asked, his eyes wide.

"Shifting. I know it could hurt, but I am never going to shift if I don't try, you know?"

"Bex," Breaker said hesitantly, "what if you end up—"

"Passing out?" I asked as Jagger watched me with blatant concern. "Completely possible, but it's worth it to me. I am tired of not knowing and not trying."

The three of them exchanged a look before Gage nodded. "Alright. Get changed into something warm and we'll go outside."

I was shocked he'd agreed that easily, but I wasn't going to complain.

"Outside?" I asked curiously. I had sort of imagined doing it in here.

"Just in case. You have no idea what you're going to shift into," Breaker pointed out. I grinned but didn't argue, going to change.

What did they think I would shift into? A dragon?

The idea, while appealing in a secret part of my mind, was impossible. There was no way an animal like that, that powerful and domineering, would stay dormant for eighteen years. Quickly changing into a pair of black jeans with an oversized gold sweater and black high heel boots, I walked back out to see the guys having a quiet conversation.

"I'm good to go."

Gage looked me over, seeming to approve. "Let's do this."

Despite our issue earlier, I knew I could trust Gage with my life, so when we went outside in the cold evening, following him towards an empty space of land behind the dorms, I wasn't nervous. I had been thinking about this for a few hours now, and while the potential pain was rather substantial, I was tired of doing nothing. I'd come to DIA for a reason, and I didn't want to continue to feel self-conscious about my situation.

"Alright." Gage kept his focus on me as Breaker and Jagger each backed up a bit. "Do you remember how we did it last time?"

"Yeah." I hesitated, thinking about how horrible that had been. It had been years ago; maybe this would be different. "But what if it isn't a sensation in the middle of your chest like for dragons? Before you said to focus on the flame there—is that dragon specific?"

Gage nodded, thinking it over. "It is. Shifters, though, no matter what type, hold their magic in the center of their frame so that it can expand outwards whenever needed. You need to find that flame, or whatever it is that you imagine, in the center of your chest and force it forward."

"Okay." I swallowed nervously and raised my voice so the others could hear. "Sorry if this takes a minute."

Oh, and know that it has the complete possibility to fail. In fact, it most likely would.

"You've got this," Breaker assured me as Jagger nodded in agreement, their support making me feel ten times better. Gage motioned for me to step back, and I relaxed my body, fully letting go of any tension or nervousness.

I didn't know what else to imagine at the center of my body, if we were being honest, so it ended up being a flame. That was what I searched for as I tried to find that part of my chest, that part of my being, that was attached to something else. Something more. And at first, much to my frustration, there was absolutely nothing. As usual.

My head began to pulse, but I'd expected that.

I didn't give up though, and I kept shifting through imaginary layers of my being, trying to find that flame in the darkness. I felt myself freeze when after a few minutes of looking, I swore I saw it.

It was so dim, I couldn't even tell what it was, and it seemed to be encased inside a dark orb of sorts. *That* was when my head exploded in pain. I refused to lose sight of it, though, and desperately kept trying to draw closer. I could feel my nose bleeding, but despite the torment, I pushed through it. When I finally got close enough, I realized that it was a very dim flame surrounded by a black shadowy orb that seemed threatening in nature.

It was my own body though. I wasn't afraid.

So I reached out and touched it. Shards of pure agony burst behind my eyes, my head felt like it was splitting in two, and I cried out so loud my throat felt raw. I didn't try to stop my frame as I fell into the darkness, the shadow orb still perfectly intact.

Chapter 17

Bexley

From the moment I woke up, I knew something was off. Not with me—no, I felt sore and my head was pounding, which was expected—but something was off with my dragons. I sat up, blinking against the morning light coming from my windows.

Had I slept through the entire night after passing out? Crap.

I couldn't focus on that for very long though because Gage was laid out next to me on the bed. I would have assumed he was sleeping if it wasn't for the tension running through his frame, and when I met his gaze, I saw sadness. More than sadness, though—an acceptance. Instantly, I knew my instincts were right.

"What?" I asked, my voice a bit hoarse from sleep.

Gage's eyes were filled with shadows as he looked

over my expression. "That can't happen again, Bex. I can't watch you do that again."

"What are you talking about?"

I knew what he was talking about, but did he mean I wouldn't be trying anymore? Because that wasn't going to be possible.

"I can't watch you torture yourself while trying to shift." His voice was filled with acute distress, confirming my suspicions.

I understood his point, I really did, but he said it like that meant so much more. Like he was accepting something, and the only thing I could think of was him accepting that I would never shift...

I hadn't accepted that. I wouldn't accept that.

"Well I'm not done trying," I countered. "In fact, I plan on trying again today. I finally found this little flame at my center, but it's surrounded by a shadowy orb. It's probably symbolic, but everything was fine until I touched it."

Gage's jaw clenched as he offered me a knowing look. "And when you touched it? What happened then, cupcake?"

"I mean, obviously it hurt."

"You've been unconscious for almost twelve hours." He sat up, running a hand through his hair. "I can't watch you hurt yourself. I can't watch you put yourself in enough pain to be unconscious for twelve fucking hours."

I felt my temper flare because his tone was so final. I stood up and rounded the bed, looking up into his gaze and offering him an incredulous look. "Well then *don't* watch, but stop acting like this is over. I can't go my entire life without shifting." I'd never been mad at Gage, but right now? I was pissed.

His eyes flared. "You're not doing it again."

I reared back and narrowed my eyes. "Gage, you mean everything to me. You know how much I love you." We'd said it a million times, but somehow this time the words seemed to make him feel worse. "But you do not get to decide this. Be part of it or don't, but I am more determined than ever. The others—"

"Agree."

The word had a finality and the ring of truth. Instantly I felt betrayal that they would all give up that easily. Instead of arguing with him, I walked over to my closet and tried opening it, determined to get to class, even if it meant being early. Before I could even open it an inch, it slammed shut.

"What are you doing?" I turned to find him standing over me, his hand on the door. He was looking over my face with a perplexed expression, as if he didn't understand what I was attempting to do.

"What are you doing? You're not going to class after that."

My patience officially hit its end.

"No, Gage. We aren't doing this. I am going to class, and I am going to continue to try to shift. If you don't want to be part of that, fine. But you are not going to stop me from doing something."

There was a dominance that flared in a magical wave off of him that had me wanting to listen to him, but instead of doing so, I put my chin up and held his gaze. A low rumble broke from his chest and he grabbed my chin, holding me captive.

"No."

"Yes," I growled, feeling like this was less us and far more our animals... Well, his animal. I wanted so badly to either look away or agree with him, but I pulled at the same place in my chest, and despite my head pounding, I kept holding his gaze. I watched as his eyes bled to bronze, and my pulse jumped, feeling for the first time an emotion I never associated with Gage.

Fear.

"Bex," he warned.

"I always trust you, Gage," I whispered, feeling more serious than I'd ever been before. "Always. I need you to trust me. I need you to understand how important this is."

When his hand came down from the door and wrapped around the back of my neck, I felt my body melt as he stepped into me. My magic flared, realizing how hard he was against my body, but I didn't move. Instead I relished in the feeling that I could affect him that much. My chest felt tight and hot as he leaned closer so that we were practically nose to nose, his lips a brush away from my own.

My head was still pulsing and I winced, feeling my nose start to bleed again. I refused to end this stand-off though.

"Fuck." Gage tore away from me, stepping back upon seeing the blood, his demeanor almost manic. I felt like I had been whipped around, and suddenly, Gage was back with tissues to clean up my nose.

I could see the softness and concern there, the heavy, saturated alpha-level dominance from before just gone. Well, not gone because he always had that, but maybe I never realized just how much he was holding back.

"Fuck, I'm sorry," Gage growled softly and then turned and left, leaving me speechless. I closed my eyes, really, really tired of people walking out.

I sincerely considered not going to class for a minute, wanting to crawl back into bed, but I knew that wouldn't help—in fact, I needed to get far away from the dorms. I grabbed my clothes and headed towards the bathroom. I wasn't going to stop going to class or trying to shift because of them.

I may have cared about them, but I still valued what I wanted.

I hadn't realized how important that was to me until now. When I walked out into the main room, there was no coffee or morning fire to greet me. Just a cold, empty space. I swallowed down the feeling that things were so much worse than I realized.

It was a thought that stuck with me as I got dressed in a cozy, comfortable outfit, not feeling like going out of my way to look cute today. The leggings and cashmere sweater with boots was more than enough. I took extra long on my makeup even, somehow hoping one of them would show up, but when no one did, I made my way to the elevator, determined to see this day out.

I know they had said to not go to class alone, but I couldn't wait around forever.

Honestly, I didn't even know what class I had until I was halfway to campus and pulled out my schedule from my bag. I looked up from my schedule in confusion, trying to locate the west training yard past the fourth-year dorms. That was where I was supposed to go, apparently. Bringing my finger to the paper, I traced the day to confirm I was supposed to go there and paused as I came to the title of the class: *Shifting with Ease*.

Well, that was horribly ironic.

I stood frozen in the courtyard, wondering if it would be bad to just not go. I didn't want to be that student, but I also didn't want to be the student who wasn't shifting while everyone else was. I put away my schedule and let out a small exhale, preparing myself to head over there. Maybe I could explain to the teacher and they would...have me leave class again? Sit out?

"Bex."

The familiar, friendly voice had me turning in relief. I smiled at my wolf friend, Fletcher. "Hey, what's up?"

It was odd seeing him outside of the lake where we'd met, and even more odd that he was dressed in a full outfit, including a coat with a bag slung over his shoulder.

"Going to the east training yards. My brother is coaching the team; they have a mid-morning practice with the game this weekend, and I figured I had nothing better to do." He shrugged easily. "How about you?"

"I am supposed to go to *Shifting with Ease*," I said, my irritation at the notion obvious.

Fletcher winced, offering me an understanding look. "Listen, I'm not one to usually say this, but maybe ditch?"

"And do what? I can't go back to my dorms."

"Why?" He frowned in concern.

"I tried to shift last night and passed out for twelve hours." I closed my eyes in embarrassment. "Now they are insisting I never try again."

I felt like 'they' didn't need to be defined.

"I see." Fletcher paused in thought. "Well, I'm sure watching the rugby team beat the shit out of each other will entertain you. Come on."

I offered a small laugh and followed him as we walked past first and second year dorms towards the bleachers of the training yard. The practice looked like it was about to start, so I followed him up the stairs, taking seats close to the front. I was instantly looking over the team with interest, noticing that the coach was Mr. Clanguard.

"Your brother is my *Basics* teacher," I informed Fletcher.

His eyes flashed dark. "Are you in class with Rachel then?"

"Rachel? Yeah, she's amazing," I said brightly.

Fletcher had a pained look come across his face. "She is."

I would have asked what was wrong, but just at that moment, I caught sight of Gage. *How had I forgotten he was on the team?* He was standing on the field, his eyes fully focused on me. I offered a small wave, feeling awkward about earlier, but that somehow seemed to only work him up more, his gaze going to Fletcher.

"Ah, I seemed to have forgotten Gage was on the team," he grunted, sounding a bit worried. "This could be a problem."

"Why?" I asked seriously.

He hesitated. "I don't know how to explain, and I have a feeling I won't have to here in a moment."

"Gage! Back on the field. Now." Mr. Clanguard's voice sounded from across the field, and I turned my head to watch Gage striding towards us, vaulting himself over the railing easily.

At first, my natural reaction was to be happy to see him. Despite our problems of only about an hour ago, Gage was everything to me. But then I saw it again. The dominance. The one that continued to both turn me on and frustrate me, especially when he began giving orders. Fletcher stood up, his posture completely relaxed as if he wasn't concerned about the aggression radiating off my dragon.

"Fuck off, Clanguard. Now. If she wants to watch practice, she'll do it without you," Gage growled in a tone filled with anger, so much so I was feeling a bit overwhelmed. Fletcher didn't get pissed though—instead he spoke honestly.

"She didn't want to go to class, so I was going here and suggested—"

"I don't care," Gage hissed.

"Stop it." I stood up, finally snapping out of it. "What are you doing? Fletcher is a friend."

"Fletcher is the future Alpha of the Clanguard wolf pack," Gage's tone was hard and caused me to lean back in surprise, not at his information but at how mean he was being. I don't think he'd ever snipped at me like that.

"So what?" I demanded.

"Bexley," Fletcher warned. This wasn't about him though.

I stepped closer to Gage. "I'm serious. *So what?* You don't get to do this, Gage. Jagger and Breaker have been clear that there is something here, something between us, but you and I have been on different pages since arriving here. I don't know if you want to be friends with me or kiss me like the first day. You keep getting angry at people and trying to boss me around. You say you want me to be happy but then say I can't try shifting anymore. I am beyond confused, and I don't know what is going on with you, but—"

My body was lifted against Gage's large frame as his large hand slid into my hair, demanding my attention as his lips seared to mine. The world exploded behind my eyelids in color as I let out a surprised moan, melting into the intense, devouring kiss. I was out of breath and shocked as he pulled back, examining my face with a darkness I'd never expect from him.

"I am not going to sit here, Bexley, and let some asshole steal my mate."

What?

Everything went silent, and I stared at him in complete confusion. There was a hard throbbing on my temples, hard enough it made me dizzy... But unlike usual, I fought past it. It felt like something had shifted inside of me, like my body was growing almost tolerant to the pain. My voice was shaky when I spoke next, pulling his attention from where he was glaring at Fletcher, having put me down and pulled me against him.

I think they were arguing about that, but I could barely focus.

"What?" I pulled back. Well, I tried to. Gage just yanked me further against him. "Gage, what did you just call me?"

"My mate."

His voice was nearly unrecognizable, filled with a rough, growled tone, as he studied me with truly bronze eyes. I was trembling, and I saw realization hit him, his dragon fading just slightly as he cursed. He hadn't meant to say that? Or he wasn't supposed to have said that?

"I don't understand... How can we be mates?" My pulse was pounding in my head. Loud. Uneven. Everything around me was spinning.

"Because you're a—"

Fletcher's words echoed around me. I heard him. I one hundred percent heard him, and for a moment, I thought my headache was gone. But right as Gage's dragon resurfaced and he snarled at the wolf, darkness collapsed over me.

My head hit the concrete, hard, as the knowledge of what he said slipped away.

Chapter 18

Bexley

This had to stop happening.

I understood that in the long-term passing out wasn't a big deal, especially if I eventually shifted—but it was embarrassing! What was this, the third time since Sunday that I'd passed out?

I knew it was Thursday before I even opened my eyes, and in that instant, looking up into the afternoon sky, I recognized that today would have to be different. I wasn't going to do this again. I wasn't going to get in a fight with Gage. I wasn't going to beat around the bush regarding my feelings for the other two men. No, I was going to handle a few very key issues that had recently come to light.

The first being the flame in the center of my chest

that I knew was the key to shifting but was locked away from my touch. Why was my magic locked up from me? My head pulsed, but I refused to let the fuzziness seep over me. Although these thoughts seemed to be fueling my headaches, I knew that if I wanted to find out anything, I would have to fight it.

Plus, I could feel myself building a tolerance.

I teased the theory with a secondary memory: *Gage saying I was his mate.*

Pain, more intense than a moment ago, began to pulse my temples as my stomach rolled. I inhaled, breathing through it, relieved to realize that there was a reason for my suffering. I didn't understand it fully, but it was there, right within reach.

Finally, I tried to remember the words that I couldn't remember but knew were important. The words that Fletcher had said before I passed out—

My head exploded in pain, so I pulled myself back from that avenue, exhaling sharply. Okay, so that...that wasn't going to happen. Not yet. I groaned, running a hand over my face. This was already turning out to be an intense day, especially since I hadn't had any coffee. I muttered a curse under my breath before finally opening my eyes and listening to the relaxed voices from the other room.

The smell of coffee hit my nose as I soothed myself with the sound of their voices. At least this was different than yesterday morning, and that filled me with hope. I wouldn't let that get messed up.

I sat up, strengthening my resolve to be as straightforward as possible. I would explain the headaches and try to explain the thoughts that triggered them.

"Good afternoon, *mo chuisle.*"

"Breaker." I offered a small smile as he began walking towards my bed from where he'd been in the doorway. His eyes were filled with both a level of heat and concern that I figured was about what had happened.

"How are you feeling?" he asked, tucking a piece of hair behind my ear as I leaned into his touch.

"Good," I said reflexively, then caught myself and sighed. "Okay, not good..."

He chuckled at my one-eighty of an answer, but I continued, "We need to talk."

His eyes shaded with darkness again as he motioned for me to stand up. "Come on, Jagger made coffee." *Of course he had.*

When I went to grab my robe, the box I kept at the bottom of my closet caught my eye, and I called Breaker back. He appeared almost instantly, but I hesitated for a moment. I didn't really know how to ask my question, so

I decided to follow my thought process of being straight-forward.

"Are you my pen pal?"

His handwriting was the same. He used the same nickname. If he wasn't, he would look at me in confusion. If he was... Well, that would be probably obvious.

His eyes melted to gold, the blue and black disappearing as he offered me what was almost a cautious look. "Your pen pal?"

I crouched down and pulled out my box, offering it to him. "Yeah. Did you write these to me?" I wasn't going to ask why or how yet, I just needed confirmation.

Emotion filled Breaker's gaze as he opened the box, and a smile slipped onto his lips that had me leaning closer to him. He seemed frozen in thought for a minute before he swallowed and closed the box, looking me in the eye. "I think you know the answer to that, Bex."

I offered him a small smile as I stepped into him, wrapping my arms around his large torso before speaking honestly. "I don't know why or how, but thank you. They made some really difficult times much better."

Breaker pulled back slightly, tilting up my chin and looking over my expression. "I want to tell you. More than anything."

I could tell that, and part of me wanted to push, but

the mild thumping in my temple warned me that it would only cause pain. Somehow Breaker writing me letters was part of this entire situation.

"I believe you," I assured him.

He seemed to try to control his emotion and led me to the living room after I placed the box back down. Gage was sitting near the fireplace, his head in his hands as he seemed to be in deep thought. I broke from Breaker and approached Jagger, who offered me a cup of coffee. I kissed his cheek in thanks, a soft rumble coming from his throat. I could tell Jagger loved small stuff like that, and since it came mostly on instinct, I planned to continue doing it.

"Gage?" I called out, and when he turned his head to look at me, I set down my coffee and walked over to him, sliding onto his lap and wrapping my arms around his neck. I could tell he hadn't slept, and his face was tormented far too much for a situation I knew we could handle.

"I keep fucking this up," he murmured against my neck. "I keep fucking it up so damn bad, cupcake."

"No you don't," I insisted. "Yesterday was a bit rough, that's all."

He pulled back, his eyes meeting mine. "Do you remember?"

"Yes." I stood up and kept his gaze. "But before we talk about that, I think I figured something out."

Both Jagger and Breaker moved closer, my cheeks heating with their direct attention on me. I decided to continue before chickening out. "I've always known that my headaches are related to saying certain things, but since my birthday, and especially since last night, I have been able to handle them without passing out. For example, I can think about that night in the alleyway, when you found me, with almost no pain"—I frowned in realization, trying to push myself—"and while it hurts to search for my powers, I can think about the flame in the center of my chest and keep focused. I can even talk about Gage saying I was his mate without passing out, although that one does hurt my head a bit."

"Because of what it means," Jagger murmured.

"Is it true?" I asked him seriously. "Am I?"

Gage's eyes flared with bronze. "Always have been, cupcake."

I couldn't help the explosion of happiness in my chest. I knew there were so many aspects to this I didn't understand, and I knew things were being kept from me, even by my own mind, but I couldn't deny the unadulterated happiness his statement provoked. Although it did make me question my relationship with the others. I looked towards them, both staring at me with a mixture of frustration and confusion, like they wanted to say something but couldn't.

"I love that," I said, hoping he could hear the sincerity and sheer joy in my tone. "But...if you're my mate, what about the feelings I have for Breaker and Jagger?" *Because I knew those weren't fake.*

"You aren't just Gage's mate." Breaker's words caused Jagger to hiss before stepping forward and scanning me in panic, cupping my elbow as if he was worried I would black out. My head pulsed a bit, but I breathed through it.

"What do you mean?"

"You're okay?" Jagger asked, "With him saying that?"

"Yes," I murmured, feeling out how I felt exactly.

Breaker and Jagger exchanged a look before the second spoke. "We're your mates as well, little treasure. All three of us are."

My eyes widened, and I realized that mixed in with the pure bliss I felt, there was a lack of surprise. Somehow, I'd already known. I was beyond thrilled, a smile breaking out onto my lips as my eyes stung with emotion I didn't even know how to process. I exhaled sharply and nibbled my lips. "All three of you?"

"All three of us," Gage affirmed.

Wow.

"I don't understand," I murmured. "How is that—"

My words cut off as daggers of pain shot through my head, and I groaned, leaning into Jagger. I shook myself and changed course. "Okay, never mind. No one answer that, and I am not going to think about it. We can figure out that part later, just like thinking about what Fletcher said later."

"He's a piece of shit," Gage cursed.

"No he's not," I defended my friend. "The part I need to know is why I can't directly talk or think about stuff without it causing a headache. I can't even try to figure it out without being blocked by the pain. It's so damn aggravating. I think I need your help."

I examined all of their faces and saw the truth —*They knew.*

"You know," I whispered.

"We can't even tell you why because it hurts you," Jagger growled out.

"Has since that first night," Gage grunted.

I looked at all of them, seeing that they were being honest, that they didn't want to keep things from me but had to. I blew air out on an exhale, realizing that the only way to get this all sorted out was to fix the headaches.

"How do we stop it?"

"We don't know," Breaker admitted. "We think shifting may work."

"But I can't shift without knocking out," I said, pacing in a small circle as I thought. "Shifters usually shift the first time because of extreme emotions or reactions?"

"Yes." Gage nodded.

"The most extreme reaction I have ever felt was flying with you, Gage," I admitted softly. "Well, that and you guys just telling me we were mates." Jagger let out a sound that almost sounded jealous about the flying, but I offered him a small smile. "There's a few other ways I imagine would elicit a strong reaction, but I don't want to use any of them for the purpose of shifting."

I blushed as they chuckled, knowing most likely I was talking about my physical reaction to them. Although today, outside of those normal reactions, I felt charged, and it wasn't until the rumble outside that I realized why. *It was storming.* The patter of the rain, rolling thunder, and lighting all hit me at once, and I realized that was the energy I felt coursing through the space.

My storm dragons' magic was being charged by the weather.

"We don't go to class when it storms. The school doesn't allow it because our energy affects people too much," Jagger explained when he saw the realization hit me.

"So today would be a perfect day to fly," I pointed out.

"I would be willing to go up," Jagger offered. The three exchanged a look and seemed to agree. I cast Jagger a smile, as he seemed almost hyper at the prospect of flying. That intensity reminded me of something I'd meant to talk to them about. I stepped back and looked at all of them.

"Actually, we need to talk about something else before we do that." I nibbled my lip and then continued, "I know your dragons can be intense"—Gage let out a low rumble that almost made me smile—"but if I ask you to not do something, or try to explain a situation so you can calm down, I need you to at least try." They all stared at me, their eyes flashing with colors I now associated with their dragons. "It makes me feel like I'm not being heard. Like you don't respect my opinion."

That seemed to turn the mood, but I wasn't done. "If I am your mate and this is real—like, forever real—and everything we are feeling is not going to go away, I want to make sure we do it right. I don't want to end up in a situation where any of us are mad or angry with one another. Okay?"

My statement was met with more stares, but

Breaker finally broke their silence. "It's very hard to not be protective of you, but I will always listen to you." He came up to me and pressed a kiss to my forehead before murmuring something about making lunch. I felt my chest relax at the fact that he would try. I wasn't the best at communicating negative or serious emotions, but I felt like that had been the right way to handle that, right?

Jagger stood and wrapped an arm around my waist, his hand on my lower back. "I promise that I respect you, Bexley, but I will show you daily if I have to."

I blushed at that as he pressed a kiss to my forehead, his voice a bit quieter as he said, "I'm going to go get ready, I'll be right back." I nodded and looked back to find Gage regarding me with concern.

I walked towards him and stood between his legs. "I know it's hard, Gage. I know you're being protective... just promise you will try?"

"I will always try for you," he whispered, running a hand up my waist. "I haven't been able to have you for so long that the idea of others, outside of them, having you—especially Fletcher and especially after our fight—wrecked me."

I nodded in understanding. "I imagine it's been hard knowing but not being able to say anything." I absolutely would have never lasted with a secret that big.

"I promise I wouldn't have claimed you before you knew—won't claim you before you know everything—it's the only reason I have been holding back. I have always felt...so much for you, Bex, and there is still so much that needs to be explained."

I nodded, not wanting to push it until I shifted. Realization hit me with his words though. "That's why you were upset, because you had accepted I wouldn't shift because of the pain, and so you thought I would never know."

An anguished *whoosh* of air left his throat, and I immediately wrapped my arms around him, sitting on his lap and pressing my forehead against his own. I felt my eyes sting with tears of frustration for both of us, for all the miscommunication and misunderstanding. When I pulled back, his green and bronze gaze was filled with so much affection it blew me away. I looked down at his lips, feeling heat replace the wave of emotion, his lips pressing to mine in a tentative kiss, as if I would reject him.

Instead I deepened it, a growl catching in his throat as he tightened his grip on me, pulling me flush against him. I let out a soft moan as he demanded entrance into my mouth, and the kiss turned far more demanding. When it finally broke, we were both out of breath, and I felt extremely exhilarated.

Something told me that this intensity and attraction would only grow, and now that I knew there was more truth to all of this? I was determined to get to the bottom of it so I could fully accept my mates.

Chapter 19

Bexley

"I promise I am perfectly warm." I didn't want Jagger to worry about me too much. Although I couldn't lie, I did love how much care and effort he was putting into making sure I was comfortable. A smile sat on my lips as he ignored me, continuing to adjust my jacket before fixing my hat, pulling it further over my ears for the fifth time in the last five minutes.

What about him though? As much as I appreciated him worrying about preserving my body heat, I worried about him being cold. Already his hair was slicked back because of the rain, his clothing soaked from his jog between his dorm and my own, where we stood near the french doors. That couldn't possibly be comfortable. Yet instead of even attempting to dry himself off or warm up, he pulled my hood up over my head and zipped up my rain jacket under my chin, turning me into a completely insulated cocoon of heat.

Alright, it was possible this was a bit overkill—I mean, the man had even tried to put gloves on me. How the heck was I supposed to wear gloves and ride a dragon? The rain wasn't even very cold, and my face was flushing at feeling a bit overheated. Okay, that wasn't the only reason my cheeks were turning pink. No, I knew a large part of it was the attention Jagger was paying towards me and how he kept touching me.

"It is far colder up there," Jagger murmured, looking increasingly concerned.

"Jagger?" I said softly as he met my gaze, his ears turning slightly pink. "Come on. I promise I'm fine. I'm super excited to do this together. I haven't been flying in forever."

After another long moment of evaluation, he nodded and led me out of my dorm, stopping on the bridge halfway between my dorm and his. I could feel eyes on us, and I knew the other two were watching us as Jagger jumped up onto the railing of the bridge and offered me an authentic, fully dimpled smile.

I honestly don't think I'd ever seen him this excited before.

Honestly, I had known that he was planning to jump, and I knew it was perfectly reasonable since he could shift midair and fly, but it made me nervous. Although, that nervousness was put on pause as he unzipped his jacket to reveal his bare torso.

A sound of surprise and maybe a bit of need escaped my throat because *holy fates.*

Jagger Silvershade was so incredibly cut and muscular. His muscles were so chiseled, and he had a tattoo across his chest that only drew further attention to the way his body seemed to be carved out of stone. I blinked, trying to pull myself out of the lust-induced fog I was slipping into, but suddenly I wanted to explore his tattoo and the rest of his body. I couldn't see the exact details of his tattoo, but it was scripted words surrounded by symbols. I struggled to stay in place as lightning cracked across the sky, and I met his pure silver eyes that were watching me with heat.

Obviously, I'd been caught checking him out. While I was a bit embarrassed by that, I couldn't deny that knowing what we were to one another caused me to feel less so. It helped also that it was very clear he felt the same intoxicating connection between us.

"Stay here, this will just take a moment," he promised.

I nodded, bouncing on my toes, eager to watch his shift. With a flash of a beautiful smile, amused by my excitement, Jagger fell backwards. I rushed the railing and watched in amazement as he shifted out of his human form and into a vicious dragon.

No matter how often I saw a dragon shift, I was blown away by how glorious of a process it was. It was like nothing else I'd ever seen. Unlike other shifters, there was nothing violent about it at all.

Instead, Jagger went from being a man surrounded by a fine silver mist, falling down several stories before he transformed into a massive metallic silver dragon that now stood boldly on the ground. Instantly I was smiling, because while I hadn't imagined his dragon, *this* fit him perfectly. He effortlessly beat his wings and took off from the ground, coming to rest his large head on the railing, his massive dark eyes filled with what appeared to be happiness.

Resting my hand on his nose, I spoke honestly. "Jagger, you're beautiful. I know that male dragons probably don't want to be called beautiful, but you are."

Instead of making any signal he heard me, despite me knowing that he could, his tail came around, wrapped around my waist, lifted me from the bridge, and deposited me on top of his back, near his neck.

I let out a pleased noise and gripped onto his scales. The secondary layer by his neck that acted like armor to such a vulnerable place were shaped slightly differently, allowing me to grip them with ease. I tightened my thighs around him, and as if naturally keyed into me, he shifted away from the dorm structure... Before taking off.

A scream of delight left my throat as we shot straight up into the sky.

The storm clouds were rolling, but they didn't stop us—in fact, the storm seemed to only help as the heavy winds beckoned us forward. My hood fell back and cool rain hit me in the face, the sensation absolutely invigorating. Energy surged through me like a lightning bolt, and I realized that this feeling was one that I wanted.

I wanted to experience this every single day.

Suddenly, a memory, or maybe a dream, slammed into me all at once.

Warm sunshine hit my face as the thump of wings flapping around me filled the air with the distinct scent of someone familiar to me. A sound left my throat, like nothing I'd ever heard before, and I dipped my head, my body following suit as I dove. Exhilaration and excitement hit me as I watched the trees grow closer...

Suddenly, a massive black dragon appeared to my left as a large wing wrapped around my side and pushed the air so I was once again soaring back up through the skies.

Annoyance hit me because I was totally fine! Alright,

maybe I'd been a bit close to the ground. Letting out a loud sound again, I spiraled as I soared upwards before straightening out.

The land around me shone golden under the afternoon light, and the mountains seemed to glitter as if embedded with jewels. It was gorgeous. It was home.

When I finally looked back towards the dragons near me, ones that were so large it was actually impressive, I knew that it was time to go home. But tomorrow... tomorrow I would be able to come out here again. Mom had promised me that.

Being jolted from such an intense memory was painful, but I tightened my grip on Jagger, wondering what that had meant. When had I ever been flying besides with Gage? Maybe it was a memory of a dream I'd had. That had happened before—where I'd dreamt that I was a dragon like Gage.

Fates! That would be amazing.

Thunder rumbled in the sky as lightning cracked, lighting up the pure silver scales of the dragon carrying me through peaks and dips, causing energy to shift under my skin. I couldn't help the smile that broke onto my face as I leaned closer to him, somehow instinctively knowing that he would come to a stop. I clung tighter as he suddenly plunged downwards, adrenaline shooting me right in the chest and making me feel almost euphoric.

A squeak of excitement slammed into me as we landed, sudden and fast, causing me to let out a giggle as I jolted on impact. I expected him to turn around and take off again, especially since it was pouring, but instead he shifted, causing me to fall from midair. I let out a sound of surprise as I landed in his arms in a bridal hold, his chest dripping with rainwater and his hair soaked. My breath caught at the intensity of his gaze, and despite the rain, he placed me down.

Everything lit up, feeling through the fabric of his sweatpants that he was hard. I didn't have a moment to appreciate that, though, because I was being backed up against the jagged wall of the cliffside we'd landed on. I whispered his name, my pulse and breathing erratic, as he captured my face between his large, rough hands.

Instead of saying anything, he kissed me—hard. I moaned against his lips as my fingers ran through his hair and tightened there, securing his mouth to my own. Heat exploded in my center as I grew wet between my thighs, causing my clit to pulse needily. I fought the urge to climb him, wanting to wrap my legs around him and grind against him. Now that I knew how he could make me feel, I wanted it more—way more.

When he pulled his lips away, he was breathing hard, and there was authentic happiness radiating off of him. "Sorry, little treasure, I just needed your lips. I love hearing your laugh and feeling how happy you are. It's my favorite fucking thing in the world."

His sweet words had my eyes stinging with emotion.

He continued, "I know today has been a lot and you probably feel like this is moving way too fast, but I just need you to know that I care. A lot. I'm not as outspoken as the others, especially in group settings, but the way I want you, Bexley, is like nothing I've ever experienced before. It's fucking addictive."

Then Jagger was kissing me again, this time a thread of sweetness to it, his lips moving slowly as if he was savoring the moment. I wanted to say something to him. I wanted to tell him that it wasn't too fast and that what I felt for him was so intense. I wanted to tell him all of that, but before I could, he stepped back, leaving me in a dazed stupor.

My gaze moved down his body as my eyes widened on his bulge. *Holy fates, he was huge.*

Although, I didn't get nearly as good of a look as I wanted before he shifted again. I felt like I was being pulled back and forth, the whiplash effect dizzying, as his magic saturated the air. His tail wrapped around me, securing me on his back before he shot up off the cliffside. I couldn't help the big smile that filled my face. Honestly, I was so captivated by the entire experience, by Jagger, that I realized once we were up in the air, the entire point of this.

I was supposed to be shifting, or at least trying to.

Deciding to focus, I closed my eyes tight and tried to hyper-focus on that part of me, the one that was wrapped in shadows. The one that I wasn't allowed to touch. This time, instead of hesitating, I pushed at it full-force with all the might and desire I could manage. I wanted to shatter the orb, and I could see it vibrating defensively as if it knew I was coming for it. For just a moment, I thought I could feel something.

It was like a burning sensation under my skin.

It felt like my very skin was shifting.

I let out a startled gasp and I tried to grip onto it, but it evaded me. As quickly as it had soared up, it melted away, and a frustrated groan came from my throat. I whipped back into the real world as we landed, and I rolled off Jagger, my body going limp as a warmth invaded my center. My head hurt, and I was positive my nose was bleeding, but instead of feeling disheartened, I felt more motivated than ever.

I'd felt it.

"Fuck, Bex." Jagger was immediately there, scooping

me up off the muddy ground. "I'm sorry I landed so hard. I thought you were hanging tight—"

"I felt it," I whispered, looking up at him through the rain. "And I let go, don't worry. But Jagger, I felt it. I felt it, and it felt amazing. I'm getting closer."

Jagger's throat produced a rumble but he picked me up, carrying me towards the elevator to go back to the dorm, and when we reached the top, I realized my hearing was a bit in and out. I wasn't hearing what he was saying, and I could barely see straight.

I felt Jagger kiss my head before he passed me to Gage. I smiled up at the man as he carried me into a warm, steam-filled room, and Breaker said something in passing, his voice filling the space. But it wasn't until moments later that I realized I was being urged to take a bath.

Bath? When did I get into the bathroom?

I blinked, looking around and realizing that I was alone. The door was closed, and next to me was the tub, completely filled with hot water and bubbles. I could hear voices outside, but instead of going to the door, I listened to the voice that had faintly told me to take a bath minutes ago. I shrugged off my wet clothes and sank down into the tub, letting my body melt under the water.

At first it burned a bit, but then my body began to

heat. I honestly had no idea how long I stayed there, soaking in bubbles, but eventually a large figure crouched down next to the tub. I turned my head and offered a small lazy smile. *Breaker*.

"Are you warm?" he asked softly.

"Very," I admitted. I was also tired, and the yawn that escaped me proved that. Before he could suggest I get out and go to bed, I added, "I felt it."

"So you keep saying." He chuckled softly. "Felt what?"

"I can't say, remember?" I whispered, feeling very spaced out. "But I felt it under my skin, like it was heating up. I know I didn't shift, but it's there. It is totally there."

Breaker's gaze filled with hope as he pressed a kiss to my nose. "Then we will keep trying for as long and as often as you want."

And I *would* keep trying, again and again. I finally knew what had been missing in my life. Not just my animal counterpart, but my mates. I knew if I wanted the second, fully, I would need to find the first. So I would...

After some food and a good night's sleep.

Chapter 20

Bexley

"Breaker," I complained, "Hold still."

He chuckled softly. "As much as I love you marking me, I didn't exactly imagine you drawing all over my arm."

Looking up at him, I offered a teasing smile. "But you love it, right? I mean, how many people do you know that have gold flowers on their arm? It's so cool."

"It is pretty cool," Gage agreed, looking up from a book that he had spread out on his lap. We were currently waiting for Jagger to get out of class before we went back to the dorms for the day. It wasn't something we would have done normally, but I had suggested it, wanting to make sure he was okay.

Apparently, today was not the day to be out as a

shifter. The Black Moon was taking place tonight, and it made a lot of shifters wildly unpredictable and aggressive. It was why any nighttime activities had been canceled. Heck, that was why my class, History of Trabea, had been canceled, our professor being a wolf shifter herself. Not that I was complaining. Honestly, waking up late surrounded by my three dragons was something that I would always remember.

I wasn't even positive on how to explain the emotions it had made me feel. Even after three cups of coffee, I had yet to be able to describe it. Happy? Thrilled? Joyous? Content? A sense of bone-deep 'rightness'? It was like there wasn't one word to pin it down to, so I didn't bother to try.

Continuing to draw on Breaker, I fought a smile, remembering how Gage had been laid out on an armchair, his large legs propped up on the bed and his hand intertwined with mine. Breaker had been wrapped around my center, his body between my legs and his head resting on my stomach. Jagger had been lying to my other side and had an arm locked around me so tightly that I didn't think I could have escaped, even if I had wanted to—which was very much not the case.

No, I would have much preferred to be back in bed, but since tonight wasn't going to be okay to be out, Gage had suggested we get some fresh air now. Breaker had gotten done with class around thirty minutes ago, and now we were just waiting for Jagger to finish so we could enact our plan to spend the entire night watching movies while I taught Breaker how to knit. And yes, that had been his idea!

I had never expected him to ask me, but I was more than happy to teach him. Maybe it was something we could actively do together.

"So, this Black Moon thing," I drew out. "Is it really that dangerous?"

"Yes." Gage's voice was hard, and I arched a brow at him.

He put down his book and explained. "It makes wolf shifters, specifically, extremely aggressive and danger-ous. Something about it really pulls their animalistic side out, like no other lunar event I've seen. One of the biggest issues isn't the aggression though, it's their inability to listen to the word 'no.'"

My eyes widened as Breaker let out a low rumble. I stopped drawing and asked, "What do you mean?"

"Normally wolf shifters are nearly as possessive and steadfast to their mates as dragons," Breaker said, "but during lunar events, especially this one—it doesn't always matter."

My brows went up. "Would they cheat on their mate?"

"Can't call it cheating if the other participant isn't willing," Gage growled. "The school counteracts it in a myriad of ways, and if anything does happen, they have taken quick action. But they would rather be safe than sorry, I think. The same thing is known to happen in the bigger cities. It's why I want to get you inside so badly."

"That's horrible," I murmured and shook my head. "Well, hopefully Jagger will be—*hey you*."

I smiled up at the man in question as he walked towards us, looking ridiculously handsome this morning, gracing me with a full, dimpled smile. Ever since yesterday and our flight, there was a lightness to him that hadn't been there before. I wanted to think I'd helped bring that out, but I also didn't want to give myself that much credit.

Maybe he had just gotten a really good night of sleep...*in bed with me*.

"I am going to finish this later," I told Breaker and stood up. "Are we good to go?" Suddenly, I felt overprotective of my men. I didn't want any female or male wolf shifters thinking they could touch my mates. I knew it was probably possessive of me, but I didn't care.

"Yeah." Gage stood.

"Oh! I'm going to use the bathroom real quick," I

called out and walked to the nearest building, striding towards the set of dark doors that led to a women's washroom. I had a feeling they would follow me, especially when Breaker called out after me. I offered them a small smile and a wave, planning to only be a moment.

Slipping into the bathroom, I was greeted by a silent space. I walked up to the mirror and adjusted the outfit I'd chosen to wear, the navy dress shifting around my legs that were covered in white lace tights that matched my white flats. I knew there were a million rules that told me to not wear white this time of year, but considering I was wearing a white jacket as well, I felt like it was acceptable.

Turning to go use the washroom, I froze, realizing I wasn't alone.

"Ioan?" I asked, finding him leaning against the wall across from the stalls, hidden from the view of the mirror.

"Bexley," he hissed. I immediately took stock of him, realizing that he was covered—and I mean *covered*—in bruises and bloody injuries. My breath caught in shock, and not just at his state, although that was surprising. No, I couldn't believe the malice and fury he was directing towards me.

"What are you doing here?" I demanded.

"What am I doing here?" He chuckled, his eyes

flashing with a manic light. "Shouldn't that be the question I'm asking you? And what *are* you doing here, Bexley? Whoring yourself out to dragons while pretending to be a female dragon shifter? You can't possibly believe you're their mate, especially since you haven't shifted."

I blinked, trying to not let his harsh words cut at me. "I don't know why you're upset with me, Ioan—"

"Don't know why?" he hissed, flashing across the room and pinning me to the wall by my throat, making me gasp for air. "You can't fucking imagine why I am mad at you?"

I couldn't speak, but realization hit me as I took in his injuries. I had a feeling I knew where they came from. Instead of being angry, though, my temper started to flare in my chest, furious at Ioan. What if he had hurt my mates during their confrontation? I hadn't even checked for that.

"Let me go," I demanded, choking out the words. *Where the hell was Breaker?* I thought he and the others had been coming right behind me.

"No." He barked out a laugh as if what I was saying was hilarious. "If you can be their whore, why can't you be mine? Awfully fitting of your position here, since I found out where you're from exactly."

My brows drew together in confusion, prompting him to reveal what he knew.

"An alleyway, really?" he mused. "So cliche, Bexley."

How did he know that?

"But since you are just a piece of trash at the base of it all, I think the dragons should have to share." He growled, moving closer. "What do you think? Why don't you spread your legs for me as well."

A scream came from my lips as he pushed up my dress, but his hand slammed against my lips, causing it to be muffled as I hit my head, having dropped when he let go of me. I whimpered as he tried to move his hand up further, but I began to struggle, bringing my knee up. He let out a vicious growl, slamming his body further against me.

"Stop," he snarled.

"Ioan—" I gasped as his hand left my legs and wrapped around my throat, hard. Crushing. I felt everything go spotty around me, unable to breathe between the hand covering my mouth and a bit of my nose and the other one crushing my throat. I tried to make a sound as he watched me with pleasure lighting his eyes, mixed with the manic energy from before.

I could feel myself fading, the room growing darker, but the real pain erupted when I felt something sharp press into my neck. He was shifting. Some part of my brain recognized that as Ioan's features began to distort. I cried out, a raspy, almost empty wail, as sharp claws pierced my flesh, a burning sensation exploding from my center.

He was trying to kill me.

I could feel that he was trying to kill me.

That was when something happened. I couldn't describe it, not fully, the picture of the moment warped by the lack of oxygen running through my system. Suddenly though, the room turned into an inferno. A scream sounded, and in front of me, Ioan's skin began to almost melt, his eyes filled with terror. My skin shifted, and a pure explosion of heat ran over my skin, causing everything to change.

My muscles ripped.

My bones snapped.

My voice, a raspy cry, cut through the air like a razor, the mirrors shattering around me. A creature, a monster, released itself from the confines of my being, and the pain that filled every nerve ending of who I was becoming brought me to a momentary standstill.

I exploded into the air, but it only lasted a second before darkness collapsed over me, taking my consciousness and my grasp on reality with it.

· · ·

Flicker (Book 2) - Available for order!

Want to read about the other students Bexley met at the party?

Deva's story - Order here!

Alina's story - Order here!

Series Within The Universe!

Monarchs of Hell (Completed Series) by R.L. Caulder and M. Sinclair

    Insurrection: mybook.to/Monarchs1

    Imbalance: mybook.to/Monarchs2

    Inheritance: mybook.to/Monarchs3

Dark Imaginarium Academy Series

    Phases of the Moon by M. Sinclair

    The Creatures We Crave by R.L. Caulder

    The Storm Dragons' Mate by M. Sinclair

    Blood Oath by R.L. Caulder

M. Sinclair

USA Today Bestselling Author

M. Sinclair is a Chicago native, parent to 3 cats, and can be found writing almost every moment of the day. Despite being new to publishing, M. Sinclair has been writing for nearly 10 years now. Currently in love with the Reverse Harem genre, she plans to publish an array of works that are considered romance, suspense, and horror within the year. M. Sinclair lives by the notion that there is enough room for all types of heroines in this world, and being saved is as important as saving others. If you love fantasy romance, obsessive possessive alpha males, and tough FMCs, then M. Sinclair is for you!

f

Published Works

M. Sinclair has crafted different universes with unique plotlines, character cameos, and shared universe events. As a reader, this means that you may see your favorite character or characters... appear in multiple books besides their own storyline.

Universe 1

Established in 2019

VENGEANCE

Book 1 - Savages

Book 2 - Lunatics

Book 3 - Monsters

Book 4 - Psychos

Complete Series

Vengeance : The Complete Series

THE RED MASQUES

Book 1 - Raven Blood

Book 2 - Ashes & Bones

Book 3 - Shadow Glass

Book 4 - Fire & Smoke

Book 5 - Dark King

Complete Series

A Raven Masques Novel - Birth of a Raven

TEARS OF THE SIREN

Book 1 - Horror of Your Heart

Book 2 - Broken House

Book 3 - Neon Drops

DESCENDANT

Book 1 - Descendant of Chaos

Book 2 - Descendant of Blood

Book 3 - Descendant of Sin

Book 4 - Descendant of Glory

Book 5 - Descendant of Pain

REBORN

Book 1 - Reborn In Flames

Book 2 - Soaring In Flames

Book 3 - Realm Of Flames

Book 4 - Dying in Flames

Book 5 - Ruling in Flames

THE WRONGED

Book 1 - Wicked Blaze Correctional

Book 2 - Evading Wicked Blaze

Book 3 - Defeating Wicked Blaze

Complete Series

LOST IN FAE

Book 1 - Finding Fae

Book 2 - Exploring Fae

Book 3 - Freeing Fae

Universe 2

Established in 2020

COURT OF RELLA

Book 1 - Court of Betrayal

Paranormal & Fantasy Series

THESE SERIES ARE NOT CURRENTLY AFFILIATED WITH A
SPECIFIC M. SINCLAIR UNIVERSE.

THE DEAD AND NOT SO DEAD

Book 1 - Queen of the Dead

Book 2 - Team Time with the Dead

Book 3 - Dying for the Dead

Complete Series

SILVER FALLS UNIVERSITY

Book 1 - Lost

Book 2 - Forgotten

Book 3 - Discovered

I.S.S.

Book 1 - Soothing Nightmares

Book 2 - Defending Nightmares

Book 3 - Defeating Nightmares

Universe Standalone Novel - Mating Monsters

* * *

Contemporary Universe

Established in 2021

THE SHADOWS OF WILDBERRY LANE

Book 1 - Perfection of Suffering

Book 2 - Execution of Anguish

Book 3 - Carnage of Misery

Complete Series

THEIR POSSESSION

Book 1 - Sheltered

✳ ✳ ✳

Standalone Novels

Peridot (Jewels Cafe Series)

Time for Sensibility (Women of Time)

WILLOWDALE VILLAGE COLLECTION

A collection of standalone novels about the women of Willowdale Village.

Voiceless

* * *

Collaborations

MONARCHS OF HELL

(M. SINCLAIR & R.L. CAULDER)

BOOK 1 - INSURRECTION

BOOK 2 - IMBALANCE

BOOK 3 - INHERITANCE

COMPLETED SERIES

REBEL HEARTS HEISTS DUET

(M. SINCLAIR & MELISSA ADAMS)

Book 1 - Steal Me

Book 2 - Keep Me

COMPLETED DUET

FORBIDDEN FAIRYTALES

(THE GRIM SISTERS - M. SINCLAIR & CY JONES)

Book 1 - Stolen Hood

Book 2 - Knights of Sin

Book 3 - Deadly Games